I0685786

Australian Literature:

A Snapshot in 10 Short Stories

Edited by Steve Rossiter

2011: The Australian Literature Review

www.auslit.net

ISBN-13: 978 0 9871242 0 3

DEDICATION

This book is dedicated to storytellers; those who create original fictional scenarios to entertain, intrigue, inspire and provide a catalyst for independent thought.

Australian Literature: A Snapshot in 10 Short Stories features the work of ten Australian storytellers. Of the ten authors six are, at the time of publication, established commercially published authors while four are emerging authors commercially published for the first time in these pages.

Australian Literature: A Snapshot in 10 Short Stories

CONTENTS

1

GONE
BY FLEUR MCDONALD

I can still remember when they walked in.
Their haggard look told of sorrow beyond what any
soul should bear; deep lines etched on their faces,
their eyes red-rimmed.
I watched as they spoke with the officer on the front
desk, who nodded sympathetically and reached for
the phone. My feet reacted before I could stop them.
That's my problem; I'm too soft. Not a good thing to
be as a detective. But it's my nature and, given what I
know now, I would do the same again. It was that
emotion - my softness - that carried me, almost
against my will, through the doors that day.
They obviously needed the personal touch I could
give, even though I had no idea why they were there.
I think it was their hands that I noticed the most.
Strong, firm hands; calloused but kind. Their fingers
were intertwined and every so often I noticed his
squeeze hers.

In my line of work it's rare to see a love like these two had. Although my heart ached for their grief and whatever had caused it, I had a small smile on my face as I watched an emotion I desperately needed at work.

'If you'd like to take a seat I'll get a detective to you, as soon as possible,' Officer Barr said to them. 'This morning you say?'

I couldn't hear the replies – their voices were soft and wounded.

Opening the door, I stepped into the front office and smiled at them. They were so focused on Officer Barr they didn't see me until Barr looked over and asked: 'Indy, are you free? These people would like to report a missing child.'

My heart sank. A missing child? That was not a case I wanted to work. So often when a child is taken they are never seen again. Unspeakable things are done to them: they are shipped off to an international sex trade, carved up for their organs or murdered, their body unlikely to be found. All detectives hate missing children cases - me maybe a bit more than the others. Mustering a smile, I walked over.

'Hi, I'm Detective Indy Sullivan.'

The man spoke first, glancing at his wife. 'Can you find our daughter?' His voice had a slight hysterical edge to it and was louder than when he'd been talking to the officer.

'We will do our best, Mr…?'

'Hatter. Andrew Hatter. This is my wife Belinda. Please. You need to find our daughter.'

'We will do our very best, Mr Hatter. Can I ask you some questions first? I just need to get a bit of

2

background - a description; things like that. Then we'll have as many people looking for your daughter as we can.' I smiled gently before herding them into an interview room.

It's our job as detectives to watch people and read their reactions. I can tell if someone is lying the second the words come out of their mouth. It's a useful tool.

Especially when my ten year old nephew tells me he's cleaned his teeth and he hasn't.

So this day, I watched as Mr and Mrs Hatter tried to take control of their emotions. I tried to fight down the fear that was consuming them, just as I had done twelve months before. It was then I knew that, whatever had happened to this child, the parents had nothing to do with it.

'Belinda,' I said, after we were settled, 'Can I call you that?' She nodded and I continued on.

'What's your child's name?'

As we sat down, Belinda held out a photo that she had slipped out of her handbag. Her hands shook as she passed it over and said softly: 'Her name is Skye. You can find her, can't you? She'll be hungry by now and I'm sure she'll be scared.'

The desperation in her voice broke my heart. I wanted to tell her yes. I wanted to say that by nightfall she would be holding her baby in her arms but the reality was she wouldn't be. Against my will, I glanced at the photo and felt my heart constrict. Memories came flooding back. I closed my eyes and silently counted to ten, before looking back at the little girl's parents.

I could see Skye in her mother. Her face resembled the little girl's but what intrigued me was Skye's dark brown eyes and fair hair, a combination you don't see very often. Andrew's hair was fair but his eyes were blue. While Skye had her mother's nose, a rosebud mouth and soft baby skin. She was laughing at whoever
took the photo and her hands were clasped together like she had been clapping.

'Like I said, we'll do our very best,' I reiterated, hoping my professional voice hid the inner turmoil. 'How old is she?'

'She's three,' Andrew broke in.

'Three?' Alarm bells rang. 'And you say she's been missing for a day?'

'Yes.' They said it in unison, looking straight at me.

My mouth pursed in readiness to ask why. Most people would report a missing child within two hours. Andrew cleared his throat to speak.

'I know it seems unusual to wait so long, but we've been searching for her ourselves. We thought she had just wandered away from the back yard – she'd been playing there, while Belinda was hanging out the washing. There's a playground nearby ...'

'It was about eight and Andrew had just left for work,' Belinda broke in. 'I'd just gone back into the laundry to get another load.' Her voice cracked. 'I was only gone maybe five minutes. I walked back out and started hanging Andrew's shirts and realised I couldn't hear her playing. I looked around and saw she wasn't in the sandpit. Then I called out but there wasn't any response.' She broke off as tears began to fall and I pushed the tissue box towards her. Andrew slipped his arm around her shoulder and I noticed the telltale sign of redness in his eyes.

'Bee rang me and I turned around straight away. We've been searching for her ever since. The neighbours…' his voice rose in urgency. 'The neighbours hadn't seen her. The back gate was shut. It just doesn't make any sense.'

'Okay, is this the most recent photo you have?' They both nodded. 'It was taken about two weeks ago,' Belinda said.

I asked a few more questions and then said:

'I'm going to circulate this amongst my colleagues and then come back to get some more info.' I turned to leave but Belinda grabbed my arm.

'Please find her. She means everything to us.'

I covered her hand and smiled gently. 'Of course she does and I will try to find your little girl. But I can't promise anything.'

Operation Room:

I quickly wrote up the details I knew onto the white board and stuck Skye's photo in the center. A couple of other detectives entered and, as I passed around scanned copies of Skye and her details, a few uniforms came in for the brief. I could hear the shuffling of papers, the click of shoes on the floor and feel the nervous energy that radiated from all of them. They wanted to get going.

'Skye Hatter, aged three. She's been missing since the morning. Parents have been out looking with the

neighbours' help, but they haven't found any trace of her. According to parents, the neighbours haven't seen anything. The back gate was shut and there are no other
means of escape.

'There is a playground about 150 metres from their front gate and parkland behind that, so the SES have been called in to help search. We've got the dogs out there too. At this stage, we have no evidence of foul play; just that a little girl has gone missing.
She is cared for by her mother, Belinda Hatter. Her father, Andrew Hatter works as a Supervisor at the local Bunnings store. According to them, they don't have any enemies and don't know why anyone would take their daughter… All the normal stuff.
Jack, I'll ask you and Pam to head around to the house and look for anything that might give us an idea of what happened.
Paul and Kev, you guys can door knock the surrounding streets. Julie, you can run checks on both Andrew and Belinda Hatter, check hospital records of Skye's birth and so on. You all know the drill.'
'You gonna organise a TV appeal?' Jack asked.
'Give it an hour or so and see what you guys turn up, but yep, that's a possibility.'
'Detective, what's the likelihood the parents have done something to her?' asked Paul.
I hesitated, and then chose my words carefully. 'I haven't picked up anything that would suggest responsibility for a crime. I'm a bit bemused why they waited so long to report her missing and about their lack of emotion. Yes, there have been some tears, but in my experience parents with missing

children are beside themselves - screaming, crying, begging. Hysterical stuff. But their reaction certainly doesn't indicate they're guilty; just reserved.'
I looked around the room.
'Any other questions? No? Right-o, let's find this little girl.' I turned my attention back to the photo of Skye, as everyone left the room, promising her silently that, if there was any way possible, I would return her to her parents.
Then I felt a hand on my arm. I knew it was Jack before I turned. 'Are you up to this case, Indy? I mean really up to it?'
I yanked my arm away and stared angrily at him.
'Are you questioning my decision making, Jack?'
'Not at all, but when you've been through, what you have, recently...' His voice faded as I stormed out of the room.
The information finally started to come in, none of it hopeful. Kev reported the details. 'Neighbours had helped Belinda and Andrew search from approximately eight forty five am, but found no trace of Skye. They'd all kept searching and it was a neighbour who had insisted that Andrew and Belinda go to the police.'
Kev flipped open his notebook. 'This is the neighbour, Jackie Short:
I told them they needed to get expert help after a couple of hours looking for her. But Andrew didn't want any help. He kept saying she'd just wandered off and we needed to find where she was. I couldn't stand that by three pm. We needed the Police – I didn't want that little girl out there all by herself, at night. I can't understand why they wouldn't call you.'

'Okay, I understand. Have the dogs picked up any scent?' I asked.

'Nada. It's like she's disappeared off the face of the earth,' he replied. 'Not a ribbon, not a smell, not a hair of Skye has been found.'

I sat for a while, turning the information around in my mind. I was sure that Belinda couldn't have been party to any crime, but Andrew, what about him? The more I thought about their reactions I was sure it wasn't them. However, I began to wonder if they were hiding something.

'What did the neighbour have to say about them as a family?'

'Quiet, unobtrusive. Used to stop and have short chats. Nothing to indicate there was anything different about them. Your typical next door neighbour.'

I grimaced. I knew it was the 'typical' ones that could be most dangerous.

'Right, thanks.' I ended the phone call and walked to the room, where they were huddled with a counsellor, but I stopped my hand on the door knob. I was suddenly thrust back to a time I had tried to forget.

He's gone,

Indy. He's gone.

I slammed the memories to the back of my mind and breathed deeply before I started to turn the handle.

'Indy?'

I turned. Julie was running down the hall towards me and I felt a surge of excitement at her intent.

'What have you got?'

'To be really honest, I'm not sure, but it's

interesting. Andrew and Belinda don't exist! Not with those names anyway. Their house is in the name of David Peck, their car in Lindsey Macka's. I've run a quick check on these names and apparently they walked out of Katherine, a town in the Northern Territory, four years ago and haven't been seen since. Skye's birth is registered and the parents' names are David and Lindsey Peck.'

'Why did they leave? What's the story there?' I asked, as nerve endings prickled with excitement.

'No one really seems to know. Lindsey was due to get married the day after she disappeared and it wasn't until about four days later that everyone else realised that David was gone as well. People put two and two together and had them leaving as a couple. One person said they saw David's dual-cab ute drive out of town, with two people in it, another said she was on the same flight from Katherine to Darwin with them. Neither could be confirmed.'

I was silent. Could any of this have anything to do with Skye's disappearance? Easy answer: Of course! Hard answer: Yes, but how?

Belinda leapt out of her chair when I entered the room.

'Have they found her?' she asked, pleadingly.

'Not yet, Belinda. I'm sorry. We've got as many people covering the ground as we can.'

She shut her eyes and sunk back into the chair.

I focused on Andrew. 'I need to ask you a few more questions. You said you haven't got any enemies that you know of. Can you have another think about anyone who would take your child?'

'No, there's no one. We're just a normal family!'

'But you're not 'so' normal, are you Andrew?' I asked quietly.

A flicker of emotion passed over his face and he looked down at the table.

'Andrew?'

'No, I guess we're not.'

'So is there any chance that Skye's disappearance could be linked to when you left Katherine together?'

'How did you find that out so quickly?' Belinda asked nervously. 'We've tried so hard to hide our tracks - we just didn't want to be found.'

'The fact that Skye is missing,' Andrew interrupted, 'has nothing to do with that, I can assure you. The reasons behind all of that are completely personal. I can't tell you why. It's just personal. We wouldn't have done anything to endanger Skye. She's our world.' He twisted his hands together and Belinda reached over to still them with her own.

'You see Andrew, Belinda, *I* need to make that decision. I understand that personal things can be difficult to talk about but in this situation the tiniest thing might make all the difference. How about you tell me what happened?'

The parents looked at each other and Belinda smiled through her tears.

'We always loved each other,' she said. 'Even as children we were never apart. We grew up living next door and as kids we spent hours playing together. I loved Andrew's outgoing personality, his mischievous smile…'

'And I loved Bee's gentleness and compassion for everyone. But neither of us realised it was love back then. We were just great mates, who enjoyed being together. Right Bee?'

Belinda nodded, then spoke. 'Things changed as we started our adult lives. Andrew worked on a cattle station as a Jackaroo. It was isolated and we didn't see each other very much. I decided that I wanted to travel. I went to Europe and spent a few years backpacking around.'

Andrew took up the story. 'I don't suppose we'd ever forgotten one another but we really didn't talk all that much - maybe a text message once in a while to say we were still around. I'd already hooked up with the boss's daughter. Bee had met a bloke overseas and they were about to get married. We saw each other one night in the local pub and spent hours talking. One conversation lead to another and we both realised that we were searching for something but we didn't know what it was. We'd taken the paths we had because that was what we thought was expected of us.'

'But when we were together we felt whole. Nothing was missing. Everything was right. We'd been in love all this time - that's why we hadn't been able to feel settled, When Andrew hugged me it felt like I'd come home.'

'I'd had a string of failed romances with unsuitable men - I guess it's a story you hear all the time. Never could find the right one. I didn't know if Andrew felt the same way and I wasn't sure I could take the risk.'

'The day before her wedding I rang Bee and asked for her to meet me for lunch. I told her that I loved her and I couldn't let her go through with the wedding. We know we acted selfishly, just disappearing and starting a new life, but that was the only way we could do it.'

'We just got up from the lunch table and drove out of town. We changed our names, our occupations and headed as far south as we could. I don't think either of us had ever felt so free or happy.'

'That's why there are no records of us.' Andrew leaned back, drained while Belinda searched my face. 'Of course, when we wanted to buy a house we needed our identification. I suppose we've half done what we wanted to do - we changed our names on the surface but never went any further in getting false ID. We didn't really ever want to lose ourselves, it just happened that way.'

I sat for a while digesting what had been said, the stupidity of it all. Fairy tale stuff. I understood loving intensely, but these two, well I can't say I'd ever come across a story quite like it.

'What were your previous names?' I asked.

'David Peck and Lindsey Macka.'

Their names reminded me of something and I stood so quickly I knocked the chair over.

Ignoring their startled glances, I left the room at a run. I could hear Julie typing as I brought up Google and typed in their names.

Newspaper articles stated they were missing and rumours started by locals had them running away together. As I scanned the articles the date stood out. I looked for photos of the spurned lovers. The papers were full of Lisa Pardune; photos, comments, statements, but Marco, Belinda's jilted fiance, even though mentioned in the reports, never appeared. Not a photo, not a comment, not a statement.

'Missing person reports came through on the 12th of April 2007 for Lindsey. David wasn't mentioned for another four days,' Julie said, reading from the screen, 'when Nick Pardune, owner of Pardune Station out of Katherine offered a reward for David. His daughter was David's de facto partner.'

'Get on the phone to the Katherine Police Station and see what went down. Get all the local gossip as well as the facts,' I instructed, dialing Kev's number. I spoke briefly to him, gave him the up-to-date news and hung up.

'Okay,' said Julie, hanging up the phone. 'Being a small town, it caused a huge scandal. The reward that was offered by Nick Pardune was also offered as a bounty about a year later. His daughter never recovered from the loss of David. She became silent, moody and withdrawn. More recently she's been under the care of a psychiatrist. She keeps searching for him, thinks she see him in places that he took her and so on.'

'I wonder if David knows that?' I murmured to myself. 'What about Lindsey's Marco? What happened to him?'

'Just went back home – Europe somewhere. He was never made to feel very welcome - he was an outsider, a foreigner.'

I shook my head in disbelief and left more instructions for Julie to research, then told the Hatters they were welcome to go home. I asked if they would like me to drive them. They ended up following me in their own car and, I must admit, I was grateful for the time alone. It gave me time to think about my son, Abe.

Gave me time to think about Jack and how he reacted to the son he'd never known and how he reacted to me now.

After looking through Skye's room and offering sympathetic words, I left and drove around aimlessly. I dialed his number.

'I'm sorry,' I said, when he answered his mobile. Tears pricked my eyes as I finally uttered the words, I knew he'd been longing to hear.

'You know it's okay,' he said softly. 'I'm sorry I couldn't help save him.'

'I keep thinking about him lying in the hospital - he was so white. I couldn't do anything to help him.' I was sobbing now.

'Where are you? Let me come to you.'

I garbled a response and ten minutes later he arrived. It was time to tell the full story. I met him at the front of the car. He reached out, but I wouldn't let him touch me. I just stood, my arms folded, as tears slid down my face.

'I'm sorry, Jack. So sorry. Sorry I didn't tell you about Abe or let you see him, until it was too late. I found out I was pregnant just after you left to go overseas. I knew you were going for three years and had the opportunity of a life time. I was sure I could cope by myself. I didn't want you to reject me again or think I was trying to trap you. And you would have thought that - you only broke up with me to go back to her, so if I showed up and said 'Hey babe, I'm pregnant, well...' I shrugged as Jack looked at the ground. What else was there to say about that?

'I fell in love with him the minute he was born. He

was a beautiful baby – didn't cry much, fed, slept, did everything he was supposed to. When he turned three - maybe it was just before - I noticed he was bruising easily, tended to cry more, was tired, and said his legs were sore all the time. I took him to the doctor and a few tests later, I was told he had leukemia and basically there was nothing they could do. Six months later, he was gone. You arrived home but there was nothing you could have done, there was nothing anyone could do. But Jack, I miss him so much. I can still feel him in my arms even though he's gone.'
It was then I broke down completely and Jack held me silently.
'Indy, you might want to take this call!' Jack held the mobile phone out to me. Five hours and many words later, Jack and I were back looking for Skye Hatter. We were tentatively okay, there was still much talking to do, but I knew Jack had forgiven me – he was that type of man.
'What have you got, Julie?'
'A Private investigators report. You need to read it. Now.'
Police cars swarmed the car park of a hotel, in a quiet street. The SWAT team blocked off all entrances and, when I had word everyone was in position, I raised my hand to knock.
'Police! Open up.' I expected resistance but the door opened and Marco stood there, Skye in his arms. When the rest of my team came rushing in, took Skye to safety and pushed Marco to the ground, I noticed he had dark brown eyes and fair hair.

2

DEAD OF THE NIGHT
BY SAM STEPHENS

David Wentworth sat at his desk, head in his hands. It had become a daily ritual; one which he seemed to perform far better than actual work.

He stared at the blank computer screen, begging words to appear. None did. He sighed, and looked around his home office. Bookcases lined the walls, full of books from authors who could actually put words on paper. He, on the other hand, seemed to be having trouble with that concept.

He chuckled at his own expense. Here he was, a critically acclaimed author whom *The Times* had called an exciting new talent, but he was completely unable to write anything worth printing. After signing a two book deal with his publisher, his agent told him the sky was the limit. But, as it turned out, the end of book one seemed to be the actual limit. Three false starts and countless jabs of the delete button, and book two remained a phantom.

He leaned forward in his chair, opened his internet browser and loaded Google. He typed his name, and clicked the search button.

Shameless? Maybe a little. Living in past glory? That was a question best left unanswered.

But reading reviews of his first book seemed preferable to slipping into the cool embrace of the dark depression that beckoned him as the wordless days slipped away.

The door to his office banged open and his wife stomped in, startling him.

There was an unspoken rule that when David had his door closed he wasn't to be disturbed. Of course this was trumped by the unspoken rule that when Sharon was annoyed at him, she would do whatever the hell she wanted. This was apparently one of those times. It was a metaphoric poker game. I'll see your *Closed Door*, and I'll raise you a *Don't Give A Toss*. She dropped a pile of opened mail on his desk, and without making eye contact, spun on her heel and stomped out of the room. He knew it was his imagination, but why did the temperature seem to drop whenever she entered a room?

The door slammed, and he was alone again.

He flicked through the mail. A bunch of unpaid bills. That would explain her worse-than-usual mood. He flicked them to the side as he checked the logo on each letter. Phone company. Power company. Council rates. Hadn't they just paid these? All the days seemed to melt into one.

The last one was a padded A4 envelope from his publisher. He got these from time to time -- an excited fan would send a gift to the publisher and the publisher would check it out, and if it wasn't a biohazard, pass it on to him. With his lack of writing performance though, David was pretty sure that if a plutonium stick turned up, they'd pass it on without a second glance.

He shook the envelope, and out fell a single object. A little wooden figurine. He flipped it over in his hand, examining it. It looked old. Really old. It was probably just a trinket someone picked up at a flea market and decided he might like it. It was a thoughtful gesture, but he hated to think of their inevitable disappointment when they found out he was a one hit wonder.

He held the figurine up to the light. It looked like some kind of Polynesian demon or god.

"I will call you Gerald," he announced with a hint of ceremony, and placed the figurine on the desk. It was one ugly lump of wood, but somehow endearing at the same time. He checked the envelope for the sender's name and address, but there was nothing. He'd have to ask his publisher about it so he could send a thank you letter.

Gerald's arrival had brightened up his otherwise dull morning, and he reached for his coffee cup for a celebratory drink.

He felt a sting on his arm and he flinched, yelping in surprise. His fingers brushed the cup and knocked it over. Brown liquid spilled across his desk..

The figurine lay on its side, staring at him. He picked it up, and with his other arm brushed the contents of his desktop away from the approaching brown tide. He grabbed a box of tissues and dabbed up the mess, then dropped the soggy lump into his bin.

He examined Gerald for a sharp, offending splinter. Nothing that he could see. He checked his arm to see if it had broken off in his skin, but all he saw was two red dots. He used another tissue and absently patted at the blood.

"You bit me," he said to Gerald in his sternest voice. He chuckled to himself. "But how can I stay mad at you?" He picked up the figurine, threw it in the air, caught it, and slipped it into his pocket.

"Let's go for a walk," he said.

2

"Did you get the package?" Sharon asked.

David and his wife sat on the lounge, the TV flickering in the darkness. The day had passed, and no words had magically (or manually) appeared on David's latest manuscript, and they spent the night as they always did: sitting on the lounge, watching whatever happened to be on TV.

But Sharon had broken the time honoured tradition, and had actually spoken to him, asking him about the package.

He nodded.

"Yeah. A little figurine. Kind of cool."

Sharon sat there silently for a few seconds.

"I think it's ugly," she said.

David laughed.

"Gerald is adorable."

"Gerald?" His wife looked at him like he was some kind of rapidly deteriorating and distasteful science experiment. "You named it?"

David shrugged. Silence fell once again, and they both stared at the television screen. David rubbed at the scratch on his arm. It had started to itch.

"I'm going to bed," his wife announced a few minutes later.

"Night," he said.

Sharon disappeared upstairs, and David continued to stare at the screen. After a few minutes he pulled Gerald out of his pocket.

"Don't worry about her," he said. "I don't think you're ugly."

3

David slept in his office that night. More often than not he chose the lounge in his office as a more preferable alternative to his own bed, where his wife's subzero aura would rake its icy fingers over his skin all night. Each morning they pretended it was because David had worked late, and fallen asleep. It was just a natural part of being an author. It had nothing at all to do with their crumbling marriage. Self-imposed ignorance was just as blissful as the unknowing kind.

David woke with a scream. It was still dark. His skin was damp with cold sweat. Moonlight flowed through the half opened shutters, and by instinct he turned and saw Gerald sitting on the desk, watching him.

"Don't worry," he said, and jumped at the sound of his own croaky voice. "Just a bad dream," he whispered to the figurine.

He sat up, and wiped his face on the blanket that hung limply from the lounge.

"Just a bad dream," he repeated.

He tried to remember whatever horrors had infiltrated his sleep, but only snippets came back.

Blurry snippets of an unfinished movie. Already the images were fading.

He certainly didn't want to slip back into that nightmare, so he looked around the room and with nothing better to do, sat at his desk. He wiggled the mouse, and his screen came to life. A blank page, of course. The cursor blinked on and off, mocking him with its inactivity.

David put his fingers on the keyboard, and without thinking, and for the first time in six months, he began to write.

4

Sunlight streamed through the blinds, and the only sound in the room was the mad clicking of David's keyboard. The words flowed, inspired by one hell of a freaky dream that he no longer remembered. Then just as suddenly, the words stopped.

He stared at the screen, considering the curser.

"Not so smug now, are you?"

He realised his eyes stung, and he was exhausted. He remembered nothing from the time his fingers touched the keyboard up until they halted, just as suddenly. He checked the word count. Eight thousand words.

He laughed out loud, part disbelief, part relief. He checked the time. It was just after ten. If his nightmare ripped him from the dream world to his dark office at midnight, that meant maybe ten hours of non-stop writing. As confirmation, his back pinged in protest, and so he decided to take a lay down.

No sooner had he closed his eyes, his blanket wrapped around him, that the door to his office burst open. Sharon walked into the room a metre or so, gave him an exaggerated up and down examination, and said,

"I see you're hard at work."

David swung his legs to the floor, and with a grin announced he'd put down eight thousand words that morning. But he said it to an empty room. Sharon had already left.

"Well at least *you* saw me in action," he said to Gerald. The figurine just watched him from across the room without a hint of judgement, but without much excitement either.

He lay back down on the lounge, and drifted off into a dreamless sleep.

5

David woke to a grumbling stomach. He checked the time and saw it was just after lunch. His body ached, and his arm throbbed where he had lain on it for the past few hours. He rubbed some sensation back into it, then yelped as a stabbing pain shot up his arm. He inspected the source. It was the scratch he'd gotten from Gerald the day before. It looked a little red. He'd have to get some antiseptic on that later. But first: boasting time.

He grabbed the phone from his desk, and called his agent, Stanley Valeant. Early in his career David and Stanley used to chat often. But as the words stopped flowing, these chats became more and more sporadic. He had started to dodge some of Stanley's calls (what was he supposed to say -- that his inner muse had died a tragic and irrecoverable death?), and eventually the calls stopped coming.

"Stanley Valeant," his agent answered.

"Stan!" David said.

There was a pause, and David realised with a hint of sadness and a whole bucket load of embarrassment that Stanley was trying to place his voice.

"It's David," he prompted.

"David, yes, of course! So how is Mr Rave Review Debut Author?"

He said it with as much enthusiasm and encouragement as he could, however they both knew it was a hollow question.

"I'm writing, Stan."

Stanley chuckled. "After choosing a career as a writer, that's generally part of the job description."

"No, seriously. I'm writing again."

Another pause.

Before Stanley could formulate his next question,David continued.

"Eight thousand words this morning. I haven't read it back, but it felt good. Just like old times."

"Hot damn," Stanley said. The plastic veneer had left his voice, and it actually sounded like he was genuinely impressed. "What's the project?"

David considered the question.

"A murder mystery, I think."

"What, like a detective novel?"

"Not really. At least I don't think so. Something darker. Something….not quite right."

"Good man! Dark and twisted is what you do best. So it sounds like you've found your new muse."

David chuckled.

"I sure have."

He reached out and picked up Gerald from his desk.

"My muse," he whispered.

"What was that?" Stanley asked.

"Oh, nothing," David said. "Just talking to myself."

"Well whatever works for you," Stanley said in his old, good natured voice. "Hey it was good talking to you again, David. And I'm glad you're writing again. I mean that. Stay in touch, okay?"

6

That night he dreamed again. Darkness filled his mind, and there were snatches of clarity that were filled with animalistic violence and blood. So much blood.

He woke with a start, stifling the urge to scream. Moonlight once against pierced the darkness, cutting between the blinds like silver blades.

He swung his legs from his lounge, and a clattering broke the silence of his office. David scooped the little wooden figurine up from the floor.

"Gerald. What the hell are you doing here? Taking a nap too?"

The images from his dream surfaced and wiped the smile from his face. Fragments of terror and intimate violence.

He placed Gerald on his desk, tapped a key on his keyboard, and as the screen came to life he continued writing.

7

Nine thousand words. He rubbed at his itchy eyes and felt the bunched and knotted muscles in his neck and shoulders make a half-hearted cry of protest, but he didn't care.

Nine thousand big ones.

That was a full grand more than yesterday, and a full nine grand more than the previous six months combined.

And the strange thing was he still didn't know what the story was about. A detective story, he'd told his agent, and that seemed to fit. And it definitely was going to be a dark and twisted tale, but there was something else about it that made him feel a little uneasy. Something hiding beneath the words that he didn't like.

Something familiar.

He shook away the absurd notion, and dropped his tired body onto his much loved lounge. He quickly fell into another dreamless, but uneasy sleep.

He sat up straight, suddenly awake, his mind clear. It wasn't a nightmare this time, but there was something gnawing away at his subconscious. He ran to his desk, wiggled his mouse and waited for his screen to light up.

He tapped his fingers on the desk. Patience wasn't one of his virtues. When the screen finally brightened, he scanned back through his story, reading snippets here and there, ignoring the conversations, ignoring the structure and flow. He was looking for scene descriptions.

Jack Stone, a heroic detective was on the hunt for a vicious and brutal killer who was terrorising a small country town. A town not dissimilar to his own.

He stopped scrolling as he found the scene he was after and started reading:

Jack Stone stubbed the cigarette out on the sole of his boot, then flicked it into the underbrush. Thick, dense heat engulfed him. It seemed to settle in this valley like a witch's brew.

Witch's brew? He'd have to rethink that simile on the second draft. David continued reading:

Jack looked at the bloody mess at his feet. Body parts littered the camping site, torn from their host with inhuman strength and fury. It was like a war zone. Or the aftermath of a Christmas Eve sale at the local butcher, and all the good cuts had been taken. He pulled his hat low over his eyes, and scanned the distant mountains. The camping area led towards a steep cliff, and beyond the grassy slope breathed a quiet, unsuspecting town.

David stood there for a full minute, staring at the screen. The town -- It was his town. And the mountains: if he poked fingers through the front blinds of his house, and looked up, he'd see their mighty peaks. The camping area: he'd spent many a night there, from when he was a kid right through to when he and Sharon spent some wild weekends there alone. Just them, their tent, and barely any clothing. No wonder the story felt so familiar. His subconscious had based the story in his own town. On a whim, he grabbed his keys, slipped Gerald into his pocket, and took a drive.

8

David stood where Jack Stone had surveyed the bloody mess in his story. The gravel parking area gave way to a huge expanse of soft, green grass that beckoned to campers, dogs, kids, and randy teenagers alike; none of which were currently present. David stood there alone, overlooking the grass, the lookout, the valley and mountains beyond. This place was beautiful. Sure, the air was a little thick here, but calling it a witch's brew was bordering on a literary crime.

The camping area has lost its morning dew, but it still felt fresh out here. While he had grown up a beachside boy, after moving to the country he had started to love it more and more. The emptiness and seclusion offered a certain peace that the bustling coast could not.

He sat on the railing and looked out over the valley. "You like it here, Gerald?"

He patted his pocket. Gerald was gone.

He looked back towards the car. Nothing on the grass. With apprehension, he looked down the cliff face. Gerald looked up at him.

Seven or eight metres below the steep drop, the

land smoothed out and was engulfed by a thicket of trees before it continued its three hundred metre plunge to the valley floor.

At the grassy tree line, he saw the tiny wooden shape of Gerald.

David sighed. To leave Gerald at the bottom of the hill would be to leave his career in the same place. Gerald was his muse. He was sure of it.

With more than a little anguish, he climbed over the railing and surveyed his intended path. The cliff face was woven with grass, but every so often bare rock jutted. It wasn't a vertical drop, but close enough to it.

With his back to the valley floor and the bone shattering drop that went with it, David lowered himself over the cliff face.

9

"It's just like climbing a ladder," he called out to Gerald.

He grabbed large handfuls of grass for balance as he dug his feet into the slope, looking for purchase. Bit by bit he made his way down. Soon he was eye level with the park area. A few more steps down, then all he could see in front of him was the cliff.

Slow and steady. No point in becoming a martyr in the cause of wooden figurine rescue.

He could feel his heart beating faster, his palms becoming sweaty. The rock he stepped onto crumbled, and fell away under his weight.

He cursed as he swung from the tufts of grass. His feet grappled to find a ledge or crevice in the cliff face.

The grass started to tear. First one strand, then another, then a lot more gave way. He imagined a fall, a broken leg, the bone tearing through the skin of his shin as it splintered.

Then finally he found it: A small fold in the cliff face, and he dug the toe of his shoe in, taking his weight. He stood there for close to ten seconds, his heart beating, his breath ragged. His arms were outstretched, like he was giving the cliff a hug that bordered on inappropriate as it lingered just a little too long.

When his heart rate finally dropped back to double figures, he tentatively continued his descent.

When he felt horizontal ground below him, he sighed with relief. He fell to a sitting position, his back against the cliff. There in front of him sat Gerald, relaxing in the grass, wondering just what all the fuss was about.

"That could have been the end of me," David told the little wooden figurine.

Gerald just stared back at him, silent.

"The end of both of us. If I died, you would have just rotted here, or been eaten alive by white ants. That's not a pleasant way to go."

Gerald didn't seem moved, one way or the other. David finally got to his feet, his body aching, and walked over to Gerald and scooped up the little figurine. Something beyond the tree line caught his eye.

A dead animal?

He slipped Gerald into his pocket, and walked toward the trees. The heat from the sun disappeared as he entered the shade, but the air was even more humid, locked in by the stillness of the trees. It looked like there were a couple of metres of flat ground before the cliff face dropped off again. David stepped carefully, not wanting to slip to his death. One brush with the
afterlife per day was his preferred maximum.

He saw the misshapen flesh scattered in the grass and trees. It was a weird animal. Mangled; covered in blood. And bald. Like one of those bald cats that he'd seen on TV. Or maybe…

David felt bile jet into his mouth, and he clamped his hand over his lips.

A human hand.

And something else. An elbow? It had been hacked above and below the joint, and discarded like a sinewy off-cut of meat.

He quickly turned, but not before his mind registered the other body parts. Bone. Chunks of meat. Human hair covering a fragment of a scooped out skull.

The bile rose again, and this time there was no stopping it. David vomited until his stomach was empty, but even then it didn't stop. The muscles across his chest and back screamed in agony as the convulsions kept coming.

10

David could now smell the rotting meat. A putrid

stench of death and decay. He had no idea why he hadn't noticed it earlier, and quite frankly, didn't care.

He just wanted to be away from it all.

He hardly noticed the return trip back up the cliff face. His mind was on the bloody mess below. He was just content in the knowledge that each step took him further away, and for now, that was enough.

By the time he made it to the car he was puffing hard. Sweat glued his shirt to his skin, and flattened his hair against his scalp.

Like the bloody hair hanging limply from the empty skull.

David forced the image from his mind as he battled the urge to vomit once again.

He slid into the driver's seat, started the car, and cranked up the air-conditioning.

The drive home was in a daze, and by the time he pulled into his driveway he had almost convinced himself that it wasn't real. Couldn't have been real. Must have been a dead possum. A whole family of dead possums.

Yeah, you keep telling yourself that, big fella.

He fell into a restless sleep on his lounge, Gerald still tucked into his pocket.

Just over an hour later he woke as a shadow fell over him.

11

"Sharon, damn, how long have you been standing there?"

"What's bitten you?" she asked.

David just stared at her, his mind still foggy from his rest.

"You're white as a ghost," she said.

"Body parts," he said. "Everywhere."

She stiffened.

"What are you talking about?"

"Cops. I've got to call the cops."

David stumbled to his desk and grabbed the phone. Sharon watched him with a confused expression.

"You're not making any sense," she said.

He waved her away as he spoke into the phone. Fifteen minutes later he was back at the lookout. He'd even beaten the local police there. The detective he had spoken to insisted that if David was to meet them back at the lookout so they could take a statement, he'd pretend that David hadn't left the scene of a crime. It sounded like a reasonable deal.

The air hung thickly, no breeze yet to dissipate the blanket of humidity. David wandered across the car park, the stones crunching under his feet. The valley opened up before him, and he just stood there, enjoying the peacefulness for a while. It was almost hypnotic.

Flashes of his dream interrupted the tranquility. Detective Jack Stone surveying the scene. Blood. Violent murder.

He finally had to face what his subconscious had skirted around for the past couple of hours. He dreamed about a violent murder that was set in one of his favourite camping spots from childhood. So he took a drive out there, and what did he find? The remnants of a violent murder.

Murders.

He scratched his arm as he considered the meaning. A stab of pain hauled him out of his thoughts. Examining his arm, he saw the scratch from Gerald. It looked infected. He'd completely forgotten to dig out the splinter, and the wound seemed to be growing. Festering. It was time to take a long hot date with a bottle of antiseptic and pair of tweezers when he got home.

Engines sounded in the distance, and suddenly grew louder as three police cars rounded the last bend in the road that led into the car park. He gave them a wave, and walked towards them. He hadn't known the police in this town actually owned three cars. The lead detective introduced himself as Detective Carol. David briefly wondered how men with feminine last names survived primary and high school. Kids were mean, and seriously, what was an easier mark than a bloke named Carol? Even if it was his last name.

Jack Stone. Now *there* was a name for a rough and tough detective that grabbed crime by its balls and squeezed it into submission.

"Sir?"

David snapped back to reality. He rubbed his eyes. These strange sleeping patterns were starting to take their toll.

"Sorry, I missed that."

"I asked how you came to find the remains."

"I dropped something over the ledge."

"Try and be as precise as possible," Detective Carol said. "Even the smallest details can mean the difference between a cold case and swift justice."

Not a bad line, David thought. He might borrow that for Jack Stone.

"Gerald," David said, then felt a little self-conscious. He dug the little wooden figurine out of his pocket and held him up. "Gerald - he's a little statue. From a fan."

"A fan?"

"Yes. I'm a writer."

The detective sniffed as he processed the information. "Anything I've read?"

"My first was called *Hell Unleashed*."

The detective eyed him off for a few seconds.

"Does it have pirates in it?"

This was starting to turn into the most bizarre interview David had ever done.

"No. No pirates. It's more about demons. Fallen angels. It's a horror," he explained.

"Why not put a pirate in there?" Detective Carol offered. "A pirate who fights the devil or something."

David nodded slowly as he pretended to take the suggestion on board.

"Could be a great twist."

"Sure could," the detective agreed. "You know what else would be a good twist?"

David sighed internally.

"What else would be a good twist?"

"If a horror writer turned out to be a serial killer."

David's heart skipped a beat. *What the hell just happened?*

"I'm not sure what you mean," he stammered.

The detective watched him closely, then laughed and clapped him on the shoulder.

"Relax. I had to ask."

David smiled and desperately hoped he didn't look as pale as he felt.

"Just got a few more questions, and you can go."

David nodded. He answered the questions in a detached and distracted voice, and then made his escape as soon as the detective released him.

As he drove away, he scratched at the infection in his arm. It was red and swollen. It was starting to get a lot worse.

12

David gritted his teeth against the burn of the antiseptic as it ate away at his infected wound. He'd dug around with some tweezers, but was unable to find the offending splinter. It had probably slipped into his blood stream and would embed itself into his heart. He was pretty sure that was medically impossible, but if something like that was to happen, with his luck he'd be the first. They'd call it "David's Splintitis", and

medical students would study his case for years to come.

"What are you doing?"

David jumped, poked himself in the wound with the cloth he'd been cleaning it with, and yelped in pain.

His wife just watched from the bathroom door, her arms folded, her face straight as if it was chiselled from granite and screwed to a living skull as some kind of artistic prank. Or maybe a performance art piece. Those crazy bastards can get away with anything.

"Hey Sharon," he said. "You snuck up on me."

Sharon just watched him.

"That looks infected," she finally said, then turned and left.

"Thanks doctor," he muttered.

He finished cleaning up, and wandered back into his office. His wife was waiting for him. He looked longingly at the lounge, desperate for sleep.

"I saw you on the news," she said.

"Already? It was only a couple of hours ago."

"A big story, I guess," she said. "You didn't tell me you were going out there."

Her words were the same old nag, but her voice didn't seem to have the same conviction. David looked at his wife -really looked- for the first time in a while.

Her eyes were a little baggy. The dark rings under them had seeped into what used to be flawless complexion. It looked like he wasn't the only one who needed sleep.

"I told you I was going to call the cops," he said.

She nodded as she seemed to formulate her next question.

"Did you see it?" she asked. "Like...all the gory stuff?"

The images poured back in his mind. Cut flesh, protruding bones. And blood; blood everywhere. His vision blurred a little, and his head swam. He looked again at his lounge, longing to just lie down for a few minutes. Rest his eyes. Cleanse his consciousness.

"Yeah I saw it all," he said. "Like a wild animal had torn them all apart."

"There was more than one?"

"At least two or three, maybe. I don't know. I didn't stick around to count heads."
"Who would do such a thing?" she asked. It was rhetorical, presumably, because she turned and left the room without waiting for a response.
It was lucky, because David was afraid of the answer.

13

Instead of taking a much needed nap, David decided to check his story again. Hunt for clues. If he was somehow responsible, he had to know.
Fifteen minutes was all he could handle. He slammed his hands down on his desk, and hissed through gritted teeth. It was all just so damn frustrating.
And terrifying.
It was time to return to the scene of the crime. What else could he do? He had to know.
Sharon was in the lounge room, watching TV. He noticed it was starting to get a little dark out.
"Be back soon," David said. "Need to get something."
He pulled the front door shut before she had a chance to ask questions.
Driving up to the lookout, he thought about what he was trying to accomplish. What he hoped to find. Nothing came to mind. But it was better than sitting around, waiting for more bodies to stack up.
Darkness had filled the valley by the time he pulled into the camping ground car park. Too late he noticed a police car was still there, and the officer looked up

as David's headlights illuminated the scene. Police tape had been strung from several posts, cordoning off the
area.

His palms had started to sweat, and he rubbed them on his pants leg as he chewed his lip and decided what to do. Not that there was much choice. The officer would have recognised his car, and so it wasn't as if he could whack it in reverse and beat a hasty retreat.

So he pulled into a parking space, and worked on his story.

He closed his car door, forced the friendliest of smiles onto his face, and approached the officer.

"Can I help you, sir?" the officer asked as David approached.

"You're here late," David said conversationally.

Just two guys, hanging out in a car park, shooting the breeze.

The cop nodded. "The forensic guys are just off picking up some lights and a generator. We'll be here all night. Can I help you?"

"Probably not," David said. "I think I lost my phone earlier, I was going to poke around a bit."

"Ah, you're the writer," the officer said. "Not sure if you noticed, but it's a little dark. I don't think you'll see much."

David nodded at this sage advice. It was a lame story, but it was all he could produce on short notice. He had to put in at least a little effort to make it look believable.

"I've got a torch in the boot," he said.

The cop nodded. "No worries, when the forensic

guys get back they'll be able to light it up a little better.

But for now, just stay out of the taped off area or the chief will have my nuts in a jar."

"Thanks," David nodded, and walked over to his car. He'd just poke around long enough to make it look like he actually had a valid reason for being there, then hightail it back home. He sure didn't want to wait for the rest of the cops to arrive, and risk more questions.

He opened the boot, and smiled at the officer, who was shining his own torch in David's direction. The cop was only trying to be helpful, but it made him feel like a suspect in an interrogation room. And that was a little too close to home for his liking.

He opened the boot and saw blood everywhere.

The carpet was wet and thick with it, and the smell assaulted his nostrils. He tried not to gag, and quickly slammed the boot shut again.

"Everything okay?" the cop asked.

Blood. In my own damn car.

He smiled at the officer, and never felt so fake.

"Uh yes, I'm fine," he said, his heart and mind racing. "Left my torch at home."

"Want to wait for the forensic guys?"

Hell no!

"No thanks," he said. "Better get home to the wife."

He slid into his car, started it, and tried to ignore the cop's quizzical expression in his headlight beams. His heart was hammering, and he felt hot all over, like he'd just stepped into a sauna.

So this was what overwhelming guilt felt like.

He put as much distance between himself and the campground as he could. Eventually he pulled over to the side of the road, and considered his situation.

A situation? his subconscious screamed. *You call finding out you're a mass murderer a* situation?

But that wasn't the case.

Was it?

There wasn't actual proof that he had killed those people. And if he had, surely he'd remember it? He tried to ignore his ever-reasonable mind that tried to point out the blackouts he'd been having each night.

He fished Gerald from his pocket, and sat him on the dashboard. He smiled at the little wooden figurine.

"What do you think, Gerald? Am I a deranged killer?"

His mobile phone rang, and he jumped.

David grabbed the phone from the center console. It wasn't exactly as "lost" as he'd made it out to be.

"Yeah?" he said, without checking the caller ID.

"Dave!" It was Stanley, his agent. "I saw you on the news tonight, buddy."

David chuckled to himself. It seemed absurd, in the situation. Stanley was sniffing out free publicity. He'd picked up on the scent of money.

"Yeah, it was pretty wild," David said.

"We've got to ride this wave," Stanley said. "How's the new book coming along? How long till we can announce it?"

David ignored the question.

"What would happen if I was implicated in a murder?" he asked. It was out of his mouth before he could stop it.

There was silence for a split second while Stanley obviously computed what his suddenly rejuvenated client had said.

"Hey, it works for the gangster rappers," Stanley said, and laughed. "You want to try and work the suspect angle? It's a dangerous path, my friend, but I like the way you think. You've got balls!"

"No, it's not that," he said. "It's just..."

Just what? You've just discovered you're a psychotic killer?

"Don't worry," he finished. "It was just an idea. I better get going, Stan."

"Stay in touch, buddy!" Stanley called out as David hit the disconnect button.

David laughed, the sound shocking in the enclosed interior of the car. It was the laugh of a madman.

"If only you knew, Stan my man, if only you knew," he muttered to the empty seat beside him.

14

David sat at his desk, yawning. Sharon had already gone to bed, and he was alone. The house was silent; deadly silent. The blood splattered interior of the car was only meters away from him, parked in the driveway. Innocent on the outside, dark and twisted on the inside.

Was he really killing people in his sleep? It seemed so bizarre. So foreign. So fictional. He had to know for sure, but how?

What about evidence? He'd seen enough CSI episodes to know they scraped dirt from under your fingernails to check for DNA of the victims. He examined his own hands. They seemed clean, though his nails were a little dirty.

He walked into the bathroom, turned on the light, and used a pair of nail scissors to scrape the dirt from under his nails. He examined it. Was it blood? He sniffed at it, but he couldn't smell much.

Doing his best impersonation of a forensic scientist, he dampened his fingers under the faucet, and rubbed the grime into the water. It made a grainy paste.

He sniffed at it again. After the overpowering stench from the boot of his car, it was hard to tell if this was blood or not.

He shook his head. Inconclusive, as Detective Jack Stone would say.

There was blood splattered through the back of his car. How much more evidence did he really need?

"The murder weapon," he whispered. If he found the weapon, he'd know for sure.

The most logical place for the weapon would be in the boot of his car. But the thought of looking at all that congealed blood, and smelling the decay, made his stomach turn. He'd leave the boot to last. Start somewhere a little less confronting. Like the garage.

Half an hour of banging and scraping revealed nothing. Sure, there were a whole bunch of potential weapons, but nothing that would cut the limbs from a screaming victim.

"Oh bloody hell," he whispered to himself. "What if they were still alive while they were cut up?"

He tried to force the thought from his mind; tried to banish the image of his own crazed, blood splattered face, swinging an axe as a hysterical victim begged for her life.

He vomited into his mouth. He kept his lips clamped shut, and willed his stomach to settle. With nowhere to spit the acid liquid, he forced himself to swallow it. It almost brought on another convulsion.

There'd be no stopping the next one.

The image of the axe remained, just like the axe he kept in the shed. In a trance he made his way into the backyard, across the cool, damp lawn, to his garden shed. It looked so peaceful. So normal.

He slid the bolt back, and it screeched in the quiet night. A solar light automatically blinked on as he swung the door open.

He kept a stack of garden tools in one corner. He moved the shovels out of the way; the rake; the hoe. The axe was gone.

He ran his hands through greasy hair. That didn't necessarily mean anything. Had he lent it to someone recently? He couldn't remember.

Look in the boot of your car, numb-nuts.

"Shut up," he scolded his subconscious.

It had to be here. He looked through his tools again, and then moved some bamboo screening he hadn't quite gotten around to installing. Nothing. He pushed the lawnmower out of the way, and shoved the grass catcher to the side. He stopped, and stared at it.

The little plastic grass catcher was a lot heavier than it should have been.

He rubbed his hands through his hair once again.

He patted his pocket, and felt the comforting shape of Gerald.

"Here goes," he whispered.

He bent down and lifted the catcher up, and stared into the eyes of a corpse.

He screamed, and then bit down on his own arm to stop the noise.

The catcher lay on the floor where he'd dropped it. The head had rolled out. Jagged flesh hung from the neck where it had been hastily chopped.

He let out a small sob, and as he backed away from the mess, he bumped into some freestanding shelves. They rocked, and a bucket fell from the top shelf. It landed on the ground, and three human hands and a forearm fell out. They were caked with dry blood.

David let out another sob, and as his vision blurred he stumbled out of the shed, slamming the door behind him.

It couldn't be true.

Killer.

No!

Murderer.

"Shut up!" he screamed.

A dog howled, and another one joined in. The whole neighbourhood was suddenly alive around him.

Well, except for the contents of his shed. There was no life inside those metal walls. He clamped his hands over his ears.

He stumbled on the grass, picked himself up, and kept walking. He hardly remembered opening the back door, didn't remember stumbling through the house, but he suddenly found himself settled on his lounge chair.

His safe haven.

He tried to slow his breathing, and he wiped at tears he didn't know he'd been shedding.

Fumbling in his pocket, he pulled Gerald out and looked at the figurine.

"What do I do?" he begged. "Tell me what to do!" But Gerald stayed quiet.

Even so, an answer formed in his mind. If he was killing in his sleep, the solution was easy: don't sleep. Ever.

It was a brilliant idea, and he almost laughed. He needed pills, and lots of them.

He stumbled into the kitchen, and ransacked the medicine cupboard. He found what he was looking for.

A pack of "wake-up tablets", a friend had called them.

His friend was a long distance trucker, and sprinkled these things over his Cornflakes every morning. He'd given them to David to survive the whirlwind publicity circuit he'd done when his first book had been released.

David assumed they were some form of amphetamines, but he never asked. He really didn't want to know the answer.

He swallowed a couple down, choked on the dry tablets, and quickly stuck his head under the kitchen tap to wash them down.

He filled a glass with water, grabbed his little bottle of speed, and headed back to his office.

He decided to sit at the desk: much safer than the sweet softness of the lounge that beckoned to his tired body. Ten seconds on those sweet cushions and he'd be snoring the walls down.

He felt the tablets start to kick in, and to pass the

time he scanned through his story a little more. The words flowed through his retinas and dissipated as his brain ignored the input. The story didn't matter anymore. He had all the evidence he ever needed. The only question left was, why?

And for that, he didn't have an answer.

He sat Gerald on the desk beside him.

"Will you visit me in prison?" he asked the little wooden figurine.

15

His eyes snapped open. With a panic David realised he'd been sleeping. But for how long?

He checked the time on his computer, but it was meaningless. Though he noticed the screen hadn't yet fallen dark, and that was on a thirty minute timer. Nowhere near enough time for him to commit another felony.

He popped the cap of his bottle, swallowed two more tablets, and took a swig of his water. He rubbed his eyes, and stared at the wall in front of him.

No rest for the wicked.

He could survive the night. And the next night.

What then? What about the third night?

"Then I'll take more pills," he muttered angrily to himself. But the question was out there, and he had to stop pussy-footing around it. How many days could he survive without sleep? And when he finally did sleep again, what then? More killing?

There had to be a solution.

He looked at the bottle of pills.

There's your solution.

"Shut up brain."
Swallow them all. And you can finally rest.
"I said shut up!"
He flung the bottle across the room, and he heard the tablets break free and scatter across the floor.
He wiped at more tears as they started to flow. His mind was buzzing from the drugs, but his thoughts were coming slow from the underlying fatigue.
"Is that the solution?" he asked Gerald. "Is that the noble thing to do? Should I be my own last victim?"

16

The front door banged loudly, and he sat bolt upright.
Had he been sleeping again? Surely not.
He felt his left eye twitch, and he rubbed it with his palm. He checked the time, but his eyes were too blurry to focus.
Maybe it was the cops. They'd found trace evidence of him at the scene. The thought was oddly comforting. He realised he just wanted it to be over.
He walked from his office toward the sound, waiting for another knock. But as he approached he heard a metallic tinkle, and the door creaked open.
He turned the corner in the hall and saw a silhouette in the doorway.
The Grim Reaper, his foggy mind suggested.
The lights flicked on, and David saw his subconscious wasn't too far from the truth.
The bloody axe.
Clothing damp and stained red.
The figure stepped inside.

"Hi honey," his wife said.

"You," he croaked. Even in his sleep deprived state, he saw her eyes were dead. Lifeless. She stared straight through him.

A saying from his childhood popped into his mind: *Lights are on, but nobody's home.*

Sharon was sleepwalking. Blood had soaked her clothes, and ran down her arms, dripping from her fingertips.

She dropped her keys on the table near the front door.

No, not her keys. My keys, he realised.

"We knew this time would come," she said. Her voice was strained. Croaky. Not human.

"What time?"

She didn't answer, just smiled.

He shivered, and backed away from her.

She slung the axe over her shoulder and sauntered toward him, her face blank.

She absently scratched at the wrist that held the axe, and David saw the scabby skin beneath the fresh blood. And he knew.

"You've been bitten," he said. He scratched his own arm where the infection still held on. "Was it Gerald?"

She barked a laugh. It was hard and grotesque.

"That weak little thing? No, David," she explained like she was speaking to a child. "There were two figurines in that envelope. I chose the more powerful one. Lilith."

She considered what she'd just said.

"No, that's not right," she said. "Lilith chose me."

Her saunter turned to a quick step, and her quick step to a jog, and her jog to a run.

David sprinted for his office, his wife closing the gap, the bloody axe held high.

He slammed the office door behind him, and pushed the filing cabinet over as a barricade. It hit the floor at the same time his wife hit the door. It rocked a little, but held the door closed tight. Sharon screamed from the other side. But it didn't sound like Sharon. It sounded like Lilith. The bride of Satan.

David looked at Gerald, who still stood on his desk. "What are you?" he asked.

Gerald didn't answer.

A glint of metal shone at Gerald's feet: an antique-style fountain pen. It had been a present from his wife, last Christmas. It seemed fitting enough. David snatched it up as he heard the first splintering of his wife striking the door with the axe.

She hacked at it again. One more time and the axe head splintered through a gaping wooden wound. His wife's face appeared in the hole, and for an insane moment, David half expected her to yell, "Here's Johnny!"

He never gave her the chance. He slammed the fountain pen through the hole, and heard Sharon scream as the tip found soft flesh. He jammed it in again, and again. His wife stumbled back, wrenching the fountain pen away with her, and he heard a bang. She'd dropped the axe.

David stood there, panting, waiting for a renewed attack. But the house was silent.

He snatched another look at Gerald who remained uselessly quiet.

David crept toward the door, one foot in front of the other, slowly getting closer to the torn hole. He took a quick peek through, keeping his distance so his wife didn't return the favour with the fountain pen.

She sat on the floor, cross-legged, and crying silently. "Sharon," he whispered, and in that moment he remembered their happier times. He loved this woman, and now a fountain pen jutted from her neck, and he'd been the one to bury it there.

"Sharon," he said a little louder.

She looked up at him, tears streaming through blood. *Her blood? Or her victim's blood?*

"I'm sorry," she croaked. Her voice was strained, but it was her voice nevertheless. Lilith was gone, at least for now.

"Your neck," David said, not noticing that his own tears were flowing.

She shook her head sadly, but smiled.

"It's for the best," she said. "I tried to fight it, but I couldn't. Lilith is too strong."

"I'll call an ambulance," David said, and started to rise.

"No, it's too late for me. There's not much of me left. Lilith took it all."

"No," he croaked.

"I need you to promise me something," she said.

"Anything."

He was crying openly now, the sobs loud in the otherwise silent house.

"Destroy Lilith," she said. "Don't let her take you too."

She fell silent, and David's sobs turned into a pained howl. The sound of an injured animal. What had he done? *What had Lilith done?*

He sat with his back to the door, and eventually his sobs quietened, and he just stared across the room, his eyes vacant.

He heard her voice again. Quiet. Whispered.

"Sharon?"

"David," she said, her eyelids cracked open just a fraction. "I want you to know…" She coughed. It was a wet, chunky sound. "Your writing. I gave you a hard time, but I've always been proud of you."

She coughed again, and a fine, bloody mist sprayed David's face through the torn door. He hardly noticed the metallic taste as it coated his lips, his tongue.

She fell silent for the last time, her head resting on her chest.

David stood, pulling at his hair, crying again. He pointed an accusing finger at Gerald.

"What did you bring into my house?" he demanded. "You've taken everything from me!"

But Gerald just stood there, silent as ever.

17

The sun beat down on his neck, and David smiled. The cool breeze soothed him, and he spread the newspaper on his lap. He hummed a forgotten song as he read the headline:

HORROR WRITER MURDERS WIFE, FIVE OTHERS

Catchy. He scanned the story, and read about his arrest. "The drug addled writer was caught loading his wife's body into the boot of his car," the story continued.

He barely remembered that night, and that was a blessing.

A shadow fell across him, and he looked up at the silhouetted figure.

"You shouldn't be reading that," the man said.

David nodded, closed the paper, and smiled. He knew the story anyway. Hell, he was the star.

The evidence against him was enough for a quick conviction, and he didn't try to fight it. The blood on his wife's body was that of a number of victims. The cops assumed it was from rolling around in the blood soaked boot. David knew better.

But he kept quiet about the truth. And not even Gerald spoke up.

"It's time for your pills, Mr Wentworth," the man said.

David took them, swallowed them with the offered cup of water.

"Thanks doc," he said.

He stood, and stretched his back. He watched a bird squawk in the distance as it perched on the sign that read, "Mount Sycamore Mental Health Facility." After the trial David had tried to find answers, but each answer he uncovered simply brought up more questions. The figurines were a set, it seemed. Two ancient Polynesian gods: one good, one evil.

David scratched at the scar on his arm where the infection had been. Both he and Sharon had been bitten, and from that moment the countdown to the final battle had begun.

He remembered her funeral. He remembered

placing Sharon's own wooden figurine, Lilith, a god of unspeakable evil in the coffin beside her. The prison guards had allowed it. What was the harm? And later her body had been shipped off to be cremated. As Sharon's body burned, so too would the figurine, and hopefully, the evil would finally be destroyed.

Gerald was the last one standing, and David was his tool of war.

He chuckled.

"What's so funny?" the doctor gently asked.

David just shook his head, smiled, and walked towards the asylum doors.

His mood dampened as he thought about those last few hours: His wife's last cough. The taste of her blood in his open mouth.

Contaminating me.

He shook his head. Did the evil live on in him? This asylum was almost a gift to his sanity. In the dead of the night, if Lilith sank her claws into his mind - if she overtook him - the locked door and the high walls would be enough to keep others safe. He'd be unable to act. And that knowledge brought him rest.

Finally, he slept a dreamless sleep.

3

THE BIRTHDAY
BY REBECCA JAMES

He wakes early on the morning of his tenth birthday.
So early that it's still dark outside. The house is quiet
but he gets out of bed and hurries to the kitchen,
where the fire glows warm and the lights are bright
and he can hear the reassuring tick tick tick of the big
kitchen clock. It's only 5:00 am - still hours until his
mother will get up and give him his presents. He
considers going back to sleep but he knows that sleep
will be impossible and that time will only go slower if
he's lying motionless in bed.
He pours himself a tall glass of orange juice -
greedy, his father would complain if he could see it,
greedy, selfish boy! - but he can't see it, he's sound
asleep, oblivious, and Sebastion sits at the kitchen
bench and drinks his juice slowly, and enjoys this
small act of subversion, savours every sweet
mouthful.

He's glad to be ten. Ten is the year, he is certain, that he will become braver, more fearless. The dark will become less terrifying, this massive, cold house less intimidating. This year will be the year that the huge distance between his parent's bedroom and his own - the long dark hall, the flight of stairs - ceases to frighten him. Ten year olds aren't scared of the dark, ten year olds don't call for their mummies at night. The two hours between 5 and 7, when his parents finally get up, seems to take forever. His mother appears in the kitchen first, wraps her arms around him, pulls him close against her sweet-scented night-dress, wishes him a wonderful birthday and calls him her big ten year old boy, her fine young man. It's always embarrassing when she cuddles him like this in front of his father, and he never knows where to put himself; his arms, his body. He doesn't want to reject her, can hardly bear the thought of hurting her feelings, but his father makes his disapproval of such affection so obvious, stop babying him Sara, he says, Jesus, no wonder he's such a pussy! and it is almost impossible, in those circumstances, not to push her away, not to make himself stiff and unyielding. And so he enjoys this unobserved cuddle, enjoys wrapping his arms around his mother and holding her tight. And she enjoys it too - he can tell by the extra tight way she squeezes, the three firm kisses she presses to the top of his head.

But then his father is there, straightening his tie, sighing with irritation.

'Coffee? Sara? I'm running late.'

'Of course, darling. Just a sec.' His mother is tirelessly cheerful, always painfully eager to please.

But this only annoys his father, Sebastion can tell, and he doesn't understand why she doesn't realise, why she is so blind to what is so obvious to him. He is only ten and he can see it as clear as day. One day soon, when

he's older, he'll tell her. He'll show her how to act like she doesn't care, how to stick up for herself. Now, he can only watch on as she looks at her husband expectantly. 'Don't you have something to say, darling?'

'What?' He sighs again. 'Don't talk in riddles.'

'It's Seb's birthday, Lenny. Remember?'

'Oh for God's sake.' His father's voice is derisive, mocking, 'It's Leonard, not Lenny. I'm not a five year old boy. And I hadn't forgotten.' His father looks at him and stretches his lips in a cold smile. 'Happy birthday Sebastion.'

One day soon, when he is big enough, brave enough - maybe next year, when he's eleven - he'll tell his dad to stop being mean to his mum. He really will.

One day.

.....

When his father has left for work - after sitting at the table to drink his coffee and lecturing Sebastion on the significance of being ten - time to grow up, son. At ten I was already working, already had a weekend job, was already helping my family out financially. At ten I had a lot of responsibility. It's made me what I am today, son. Successful. Hard-working. Capable. It's time to start showing your mettle son, time to start showing some strength of character, some initiative, time to stop hiding behind your mother's skirts! - his mother tells him to go and get dressed.

'I want to show you your present,' she says.

'Can't I have it now? Do I have to get dressed?' He can argue with his mother when his father isn't around, they can be normal with each other, happy and relaxed.

'Well,' she giggles, 'It's just that we have to go for a bit of a walk, outside. You'll need some shoes, at least.'

'Come with me then,' he says. 'And I'll get my slippers.' His mother doesn't mind that he wants her to come with him, she doesn't mind that he hates walking through the house alone. In fact she seems happy to be with him, to hold his hand through the corridors and hallways. It's such a big house, an enormous house, and the ceilings are high, the floors tiled in a cold polished marble. It is still and dark and full of shadows.

His friends all have normal houses. Small and warm and cosy and full of stuff. They have carpet on the floors and when the television is on you can hear it throughout the entire house. Sebastion's house is full of emptiness and silence and when he is alone in his bedroom - which is almost as large as some of his friends' houses - he is sometimes afraid that he is the only person left alive in the world.

He gets his slippers on and his mother takes him down to the back of the garden, down behind the swimming pool and tennis court, towards the thick screen of conifers which hide the very southern corner of the garden.

'Okay,' she says, as they reach the conifers, 'close your eyes.'

'Aw mum,' he protests. 'I'm not a baby.' But he doesn't really mind doing as she asks, the truth is he loves her enthusiasm, the joy she gets from surprising him.

He closes his eyes and she takes his hand, leads him slowly around the conifers.

'Okay,' she says. 'You can look now.'

What used to be a grassy area, overgrown with shrubs, has been cleared. There's a new dirt path, which goes around in a rough oval shape, with small hills and bumps along it.

He is not sure what he's seeing at first, not sure how this relates to him. But his mother puts her hands on his shoulders and swings him around so that he is facing two new BMX bikes, both standing upright on their stands.

'It's a bike path, darling. Just for you. And a new bike.'

'Wow,' he says. It's hard to keep the disappointment from his voice. He doesn't like bike-riding. Never has. He is not a physically active boy. He prefers indoor pursuits - playing video games, watching movies, listening to music. He likes new clothes. He is cautious with his body, always has been, he doesn't like bruises and scrapes, hates hurting himself. He has never liked getting dirty.

'It was all your father's idea,' she says. 'The track. The bikes. He thought of everything. He even organised the excavator himself.'

'But why two?' Sebastion asks, puzzled. He has no idea what he is supposed to do with two bikes. One is more than enough.

'I know,' she says, clapping her hands together, her voice deliberately bright. 'He got one for Cooper too. So that you'd have someone to play with. Wasn't that a good idea? And you can invite Cooper around for the afternoon.'

His mother annoys him when she acts like this. When she pretends that everything is okay – pretends not to notice that he is disappointed or upset. She knows that he doesn't like bikes, that he is no good at riding. She must know that this is a present that will not make him happy.

'We're just going to have the most lovely day. I've organised a picnic and a big chocolate cake and you and Cooper can spend the afternoon riding and daddy will be home early in the afternoon and then we can all have a lovely dinner together.'

And so she goes on - pretending, pretending, pretending.

…

He does end up having a good day, at least the first half of it, until his dad gets home. He and his mother and Cooper have a picnic by the pool - all his favourite foods - junk, as his mother calls it - frankfurts and sausage rolls followed by the best chocolate mud cake he's ever had and as much creaming soda as they can drink. Then they muck around in the pool, and though Cooper is the much sportier of the two, he is chunkier, taller, stronger, better than Seb at nearly everything physical, Sebastion discovers that he can beat him in a long-distance freestyle race. Cooper always starts out ahead, but he splashes too much, gets fatigued early, and Sebastion eventually overtakes. Sebastion loves winning, it gives him a rarely felt and heady rush of pride, and probably because it's his birthday Cooper generously agrees to race him again and again. Loses over and over.

His mother eventually tells them to stop, to get out of the water. You'll get sick, she warns, cramps, all that junk food. Get out and lie in the sun for a while. Rest. She stands at the edge of the water with towels - first wraps Cooper, ruffles his hair fondly. Then she wraps a big towel around Sebastion and kisses him on the head. 'You're a wonderful swimmer, darling,' she says proudly.' Just like me. You have the right body type.'

Sebastion is thin and rangy. He looks like his mother. They are both dark, olive skinned, with thick mops of straight black hair that flop forward over their dark, deep-set eyes. His mother's grandparents came from Iran, a fact that his mother doesn't often talk about. Sebastion looks nothing at all like his father, who is short and stocky, nuggety with muscle, and has fair hair, cut short, close to his scalp. A fair dinkum Aussie he likes to boast when he is drinking beer, 'One-hundred percent. My ancestors came over with the first fleet. You couldn't get more Aussie than that if you tried.' And then he likes to grab Sebastion around his bicep and squeeze. 'As puny as a girl. Just like your mother,' he says. 'Not much of me in you, is there, not much Aussie, eh? A little Arab, that's what you are, eh?

Mummy's little Arab boy.'

'Not Arab,' his mother says quietly. 'Persian. There's a difference.'

Sebastion isn't even really sure what the words mean, Arab, Persian, he only knows that it is better to have blonde hair than brown, better to be strong than weak - that he, Sebastion, is all wrong.

…

When his father gets back home from work Sebastion and Cooper are still in the pool.

'Why don't you two boys have a race?' He demands, almost immediately. 'Two laps. Come on. From this end.'

When his father makes a suggestion like that there isn't really any choice, saying no isn't an option. Sebastion watches him stride to one end of the pool, cross his arms over his chest, look down at them seriously. He waits for both boys to make their way to the edge. Cooper is co-operative, cheerful, grinning. For him this is just a game, a bit of fun. But two laps isn't enough for Sebastion to gain his advantage, he knows that. Cooper will win and his father will see him as a weak loser once again. He would suggest a longer race - ten laps preferably - but his father doesn't give him the chance. Ready set Go! He shouts, and they are

off before Sebastion has a chance to suggest anything. Of course, Cooper wins, beats Sebastion by a full body-length. As if that isn't enough humiliation, his father insists that the boys get dressed and head down to the bike-path. Sebastion trudges down unhappily, a few steps behind Cooper and his father, who are both oblivious to Sebastion's increasingly bitter mood. Cooper walks right next to Sebastion's father -

cheerfully answering every gruff and demanding question Sebastion's father throws at him. He chats freely about the surf, about his mother, about school. He is natural and relaxed with Sebastion's father in a way that Sebastion never can be. With his father Sebastion is stiff and anxious, unable to be himself. Sebastion feels ridiculous on the bike, embarrassed by his own ungainliness and timidity, his inability to fly over the humps as freely as Cooper does.

Cooper rides with a reckless joyful wildness, and his lack of fear makes him graceful and balanced and fast.

Compared to Cooper, Sebastion feels weak and pathetic and clumsy but he works hard to hide his shame. He fights the urge to cry and stamp his feet or throw his

bike down in a baby-like tantrum, he does his best to be a good sport, a good loser, as his father has told him he should always be. He has become very good at acting indifferent, at being cool.

And despite his own keen disappointment with the bike-track, he wants his father to think that he is pleased with the gift - he couldn't stand to make his father unhappy, couldn't bear to see him disappointed.

And he is concerned that his own lack of skill will disappoint his father, make him ashamed. But when his father suggests the boys race twice around the track - and Cooper flies ahead, leaving Sebastion wobbling clumsily behind him - he's confused by the expression on his father's face. Cooper has beaten him, has left him in the dust, but his father is smiling.

By the end of the day he is sick to death of Cooper and can't wait for him to go home.

4

VENGEANCE
BY JJ COOPER

Chase Johns drew the razor across his twelve-year-old daughter's throat. A precise cut. It needed to be. The passport-sized photo had aged and tattered at the edges. He finished trimming and placed it back on the dash of his van. His daughter's angelic portrait never lost the ability to induce a myriad of emotions: vengeance knew no bounds for a father of a daughter lost.

An approaching set of headlights focused on the gentle summer rain cascading down the van's windshield. Chase checked his watch and turned off the interior light. He stepped into the rain and waited for his prey.

Two months of preparation to bring his plan to fruition. Most of his time spent swapping emails; acting like a love-struck teenage girl. Countless hours in chat rooms with *his* Romeos: a nineteen-year-old fitness trainer with rippling abs and a twenty-two-year-old virgin with an ear for classical music; or so they claimed.

In the rear of the van, Vince Price, a fifty-six-year-old solicitor with abs lost behind flaccid

rolls, lay bound and gagged; sedated by the pistol grip of a Glock 17. Not quite the mould of a fitness trainer he'd claimed to be online. Soon to be joined by sixty-two-year-old Davis Wiltshire, a local magistrate who would hardly have been a virgin, but may well have a taste for classical music.

The headlights of Wiltshire's BMW disappeared as it descended the undulating country lane, then reappeared and fought through the rain as the car climbed a crest.

Chase deployed a set of road spikes on his side of the hill.

They worked a treat.

It was just sixteen minutes from the moment the BMW hit the spikes until Chase had bound and gagged Wiltshire then thrown him in the back of the van. The Glock was again handy in the anaesthetist role. The process was almost two minutes quicker than the capture of the solicitor.

Chase thought about ways to improve the procedure as he drove toward a disused industrial estate on the edge of the desolate mid-western town.

Flecked rust in the shed's roof lining channeled the rain. The rust a result of years of neglect, or rather abandonment. The shed smartly erected long ago to support a short-lived mining boom. Its contents and workforce moved on to the next town when the charcoal gold ran out. It seemed only the rats, who had claimed the shed as a sanctuary, would enjoy the musky smell as it broke through the humidity.

A quiet thud echoed as Chase jumped out of his van and landed on the concrete. In the beam of the van's headlights, three metal chairs waited for occupation: set in a triangular formation with a six-foot wooden a-frame standing in the middle. Three pieces of rope wormed over the top of the frame and crept to the chairs. Each piece of rope fixed to an elaborate adaptation of a cigar cutter; ready to be strategically placed over those parts the Romeos valued so much.

Due to the disparate difference in size of his prisoners, Chase decided he could make light work of Wiltshire and commenced hauling the obese Price from the van. As he dragged Price along the concrete, it occurred to him that the weight difference between his prisoners could explain why he had taken two minutes less in the capture of the thin Magistrate - something to ponder when he compiles his after-action review.

After he'd finished preparing Price, Chase wiped sweat from his brow. Hauling the obese solicitor and attaching the cigar cutter was all the more difficult when the pedophile had awoke from his slumber during the fastening process. Fortunately, he'd already been secured to the chair and his muffled screams hardly breached the gag. Wiltshire, on the other hand, had remained unconscious until after the device had
been fitted and therefore the process was more 'routine'.

Not long before the two prisoners thrashed their

heads around like long-haired youth at a heavy-metal concert. Chase let them waste their energy and returned to the van. He grabbed a bag of carrots he'd purchased for testing the adapted cigar-cutters. Time for another test.

The head-thrashing stopped as Chase returned and sat in the vacant chair. Curiosity got the better of the Romeos. They were somewhat wide-eyed and concentrating on the carrot Chase held; perhaps more concerned about what Chase would be doing with the carrot rather than the cigar cutters. It seemed an impossible accomplishment, but their eyes widened as Chase placed the carrot in the third device, positioned it near his groin and reached forward. He pulled on the end of the rope dangling from the a-frame and connected to his cutter. The guillotine sliced true.

Price's head rolled back and his stomach lurched with his sobs. Wiltshire's head dropped and Chase hoped the older man hadn't had a heart attack.

Chase picked up the dissected carrot from the floor and gave it a wipe. He was about to take a bite, and then thought better of it, tossing it toward some scurrying rats. The stench of urine quickly overtook the damp of the shed and a puddle formed under Price.

Wiltshire came to under the guiding hand of Chase. Probably five or six slaps too many, but ultimately he was alert and staring ahead. A couple of minutes later both men were shaking, and paying attention.

Chase gave them a look of disgust and said, 'I know a man who six months ago was happily married.

Well-paid job, loving wife and a beautiful teenage daughter. Living the dream.' He started to attach the two remaining pieces of rope, that dangled over the a-frame, to a metal o-ring. The o-ring was painted gold like a wedding ring and about the size of Chase's hand.

'It all came crashing down the day his daughter took her own life.' He paused for effect, took a deep breath, pictured the saintly face of his daughter and continued. 'He couldn't comprehend why such a talented young woman with so much to look forward to in life would do such a thing.'

Chase finished tying the pieces of rope to the o-ring. 'The man's wife insisted on leaving their daughter's room untouched. The man never entered the room. Seemed like his wife never left it. She insisted it remain the same right up to the day she too killed herself.'

Chase lowered his voice. 'Just two months ago.' Another deep breath and he bit at his lip. 'In less than six months, the man had lost everything.'

He forced a hand in his pocket and said, 'Before she took her own life, the man's wife discovered their daughter's diary. A record that detailed the systematic online exploitation by you two!' He narrowed his eyes and held an accusing hand toward the bound men. 'The daughter's last entry told of her brutal rape by three men, right here in this rat-infested shed.' Spittle left his lips as he strained to get the words out. Chase put his hand on the o-ring. 'Although the three rapists weren't named, you two were easy enough to track through your online usernames from previous entries in the diary. But, the third person was never mentioned. So, who wants to speak first? And who wants half of their dick fed to the rats?'

Both men nodded with vigour.

Chase pointed a finger at Price. 'Eeny, meeny, miny, moe. Catch, a …, rapist, by, the, toe. If, he, hollers, let, him, go. Eeny, meeny, miny, moe.' His pointed at Wiltshire. Price shook his head and roared behind his gag. The noise stopped as soon as Chase continued. 'My, daughter, says, that, you, are, it.' His finger now pointed to Price. The transformation amazed Chase. He could have sworn Price was grinning behind

the duct tape.

'You know, Price. Ninety-nine percent of solicitors give the rest a bad name.' He stepped forward and ripped off the duct tape.

Price didn't wait for the pain of the tape removal to register. 'I've got money. You can have it all. Everything. Just let me go. Please. Whatever you want.'

Chase stepped back and grabbed the o-ring. It had an immediate impact. Silence.

'Who's the third person?'

Sweat ran down the fat man's face and pooled in his heavy rolls. 'I … I honestly don't know. You got to believe me. I was set up. I was emailing the girl ….'

'Kylie.'

Price shook his head as if to clear it. 'What?'

'Kylie. That's her name. Kylie.'

Price gave a slow nod. 'Kylie. We exchanged emails for a while, then I didn't hear from her for maybe a month or so. Out of the blue she sent me a message that said she would like to meet up. It was a Friday night and she wanted to meet here. I … I was concerned for her safety ….'

Chase put pressure on the o-ring. It was Wiltshire's turn to wet himself.

'No … no!' Price wanted to correct his story. 'She was beautiful. I admit I wanted her. Her message said she would be here waiting for me.'

'And?'

'It said she knew that I was older and that it didn't matter. She just wanted to make love.'

'You a good solicitor?'

'Pardon?'

'A good solicitor?'

'I suppose.'

'Of course you are. Because you're a good liar!'

'No … no ….'

Chase wrapped the duct tape back over Price's mouth and ripped the gag from Wiltshire.

'Your turn, Your Honour.'

Wiltshire sucked in deep breaths. After calming himself, he looked Chase in the eyes. 'Everything he said happened to me. I did exactly the same. She … Kylie was here. On the floor, waiting.'

'What did she say when you arrived?'

'Nothing. She appeared to be under the influence of some kind of drug.'

'Don't you think it odd, Judge, that Kylie was all the way up here, by herself, stoned, and just laying amongst the rats waiting for you?'

'Of course I did. But ….'

'But you're a sick asshole who couldn't help

himself. And you don't know who the third person is?'

Wiltshire dropped his gaze and nodded. It coincided with a set of headlights reaching for the doorway of the shed.

Chase checked his watch. Right on time. He smacked the tape back over Wiltshire's mouth and sunk into the darkness.

The police cruiser breached the shed's threshold and stopped short of the two with their *'masculinity'* in a bind.

As expected, the local police Sergeant opened his door, and with one leg in the car, looked over the doorframe, as if it would give him a better picture of the event. He reached for his radio. The Glock jammed behind his ear before he made the call.

'Good of you to join us, Sarg.'

The Police Sergeant raised his hands and Chase pushed him away from the car. Chase took the shotgun from its straddle and used it to dig into the Sergeant's back.

Chase indicated with the shotgun toward the vacant chair. 'Have a seat, Sarg.'

'I have backup on the way.'

'And I had an affair with Princess Diana. We may both be telling the truth, but it's unlikely. Move!'

As soon as the police chief sat down he said,

'Vince ... Davis. What ... what the hell is going on? And what is that on their ....'

'Little fellows, Chase said. 'Want to see a demonstration?'

Chase used the Police Officer's handcuffs to secure him to the chair and noticed Price and Wiltshire shaking their heads violently. 'I meant a demonstration with another carrot.'

Both men stopped shaking their heads and lowered them in unison.

'I'm hazarding a guess you're a bit brighter than these two. Tell me about the night six months ago where an innocent little girl was brutally raped, right here.'

'You don't have to do this, son. Don't take matters into your own hands. Let the law deal with it.'

'I step in where the law fails. Again, six months ago?' Chase raised the shotgun.

The Sergeant paused, no doubt considering his options. 'I came here on my routine patrol, picked up a teenager, who was heavily under the influence of drugs, and took her home.'

'Kylie.'

'What.'

'Her name. Kylie.'

'Yep, Kylie. Now put down the weapon, son, and it'll work out. I'll investigate your claims.'

'Sarg, from your efforts to date, you'd obviously have a hard enough time running a bath let alone an investigation.'

'There was no need for an investigation. It seemed like she'd been partying and had come up here with some boys. The boys had clearly taken off. She was high on something. Wrong place, wrong time. Nothing
I could do.'

'She was raped by three men.'

'She probably had consensual sex with some boys.

She didn't mention anything to me about any rape. And no complaint has ever been filed.'

Chase felt the anger rise. He stepped closer and poked the shotgun into the Police Sergeant's chest. 'She was raped. By three men!'

Price started bouncing his legs around and shaking his head from side to side.

'Got something you want to say, Price?'

A vigorous nod.

Chase moved toward Price.

'I wouldn't believe him,' the police officer said.

Chase paused and looked back. 'Got something to add, Sarg?'

'He's a grubby lawyer. Can't be trusted. Neither of them can.'

'That why you've managed a near perfect crime clearance rate in the last few months?'

'What's that supposed to mean?'

'I'll let Price tell me.' He ripped the gag from Price and then placed it over the Police Sergeant's mouth. 'What is it, Price?'

'We've been paying him money for nearly six months. At least I have.'

Chase looked to the o-ring and then back to Price.

'Think you could have mentioned this before?' He looked to Price's crotch. 'You can't afford to be losing any inches.'

'I didn't think it mattered. It was obvious he set us up. There was nothing I could do about it. He had it all on video.'

'A video of you raping Kylie?'

'We made love.'

Chase grabbed the o-ring.

'Ok … ok … it may appear to be like a rape on the video. But ….'

Chase held up the shotgun in a gesture to silence Price. It worked. 'You're a sick bastard, Price.' He turned to Wiltshire. 'A video exist of you too?'

A nod.

It was the Police Sergeant's turn to roar into the duct tape and shake his head wildly. Chase studied him closely then turned his attention back to Price. 'Tell me about the payments.'

'A thousand dollars a month in cash. I dropped it off here the last Friday of every month.'

'Morning or afternoon?'

'In the morning.'

Chase looked to Wiltshire. 'Let me guess. You've got the afternoon drop, your Honour?'

Another nod.

The Police Sergeant continued his animated protest.

Chase continued to question Price. 'How did the blackmailing commence?'

'The video came in the mail with instructions for the payments.'

'Signed by the Sarg here?'

'No, it was Anonymous. But it was obviously from him.' A nod toward the police officer. 'Everybody in town knows he drives by here every Friday night. That's how he found the … Kylie.'

Chase's mind raced. He went to his van and retrieved more duct tape. After fixing another length of tape to Price, he placed a call.

Twenty minutes later an agitated man walked into the fray.

Harry Larter took it all in and the stood under the a-frame. The o-ring within reach. 'These the ones who caused my little girl to take her own life? These the ones who violated my Kylie.'

'They're the ones.'

'What are you going to do to them?'

'Hand them over to the proper authorities.'

In a handwritten note to Chase, sent the day before her suicide, Mrs Larter had pleaded with Chase to track down her daughter's rapists. Chase had never met her.

He assumed she had heard about his own missing daughter and figured, because Chase was a private investigator, he could find them and bring them to justice. She had specified three people as responsible, but had only provided the two online pseudonyms to work with. Names found in her daughter's diary. Harry Larter had assumed Chase had read about the incident and had offered his services. Chase now knew why Mrs Larter hadn't told her husband the reasoning for seeking out Chase before she took her own life.

Larter's hands were by his side. 'We should kill them. Kill them for Kylie. That's what my wife would have wanted.'

'They're not worth it, Harry. They'll suffer behind bars. You don't need to join them. Your wife wanted justice for Kylie.' Chase was baiting.

'I have nothing left because of these bastards. I don't care what happens to me. They have to pay for what they did.'

'They will.'

'I thought you'd understand, Chase. How long has your daughter been missing? Three years?'

Chase shook his head. 'I haven't found my daughter yet, or the ones responsible for her disappearance. And, not a day goes by that I don't fantasise about the things I'll do to those responsible.'

'Then you know I need to kill them.'

'No. Let the system take care of them. And I don't mean the justice system. Make them suffer.'

The Police Sergeant was agitated, bumping around in his chair as best he could. Price and Wiltshire stared at the o-ring.

Chase swung the shotgun and pointed it at Larter.

'What are you doing?' Larter asked.

'Here's the thing, Harry. You want to kill them. What satisfaction is there in that? I'm guessing you've figured out those things on their dicks are cutters. One pull of that ring and it chops them straight off. Now, that's what I'd do. I think that's what any father would want to do. Make them suffer before they die. That and a whole lot more. It's all about vengeance. You just want to kill them.'

Larter looked nervous. 'That's what I meant. Make them suffer.'

'No you didn't and I know why. And, your wife knew why.'

Larter looked toward the o-ring then to the shotgun.

'Don't do it,' Chase said. 'Teenage girls looking for love online aren't that social in person. No way would she have been up here with a couple of boys. But, the Sarg here wouldn't have known that. Just assumed she was like the rest of the local girls.

76

Maybe it's because she couldn't go partying with the other girls that's why she went online. She wasn't allowed out was she?'

The nervous look from Larter had turned to anger. 'Do know what kind of things they do at that age?'

'And, as you've discovered, if they're not allowed out, they'll do it online.'

'Her emails were disgusting. Some of the things she was saying to these ... these animals.' He waved a hand at Price and Wiltshire. His hand came to rest on the o-ring.

Chase gave a small shake of his head. 'But, these two were probably just fulfilling their sick fantasies online. That changed when you initiated contact.'

'She deserved to be punished!'

'So you drugged her and brought her here to be raped. Recorded it all to punish her. Knew the Police Sergeant would be stopping by to check things out. Like he always did. You then decided you could make some money from it by blackmailing these two. Your wife found the diary. She knew there were three rapists.

Your wife figured it out and took her own life. You were responsible for it all. You watched these two rape your little girl. She was so drugged up that you figured she wouldn't remember there being three men who raped her. You were the third rapist!'

A hot breeze blew through the silence. Chase held Larter's stare. He knew what was coming.

Larter closed his eyes and pulled the ring.

Two pins flew into the air as the cigar cutters were engaged. Price flung his chair backward and landed heavily on the concrete. Wiltshire stared at his crotch and then feinted. Both men with penises intact. Only the demonstration cigar-cutter had blades.

Chase undid the handcuffs from the Police Sergeant and removed his duct tape. The police officer stood up and assessed the picture before him. Chase handed back the shotgun and helped bundle the threemen into the back of the police cruiser.

His job done, Chase climbed back into his van after promising to drive to the police station and give a full statement to the very angry Police Sergeant. He had no intention of doing so - far too many legal minefields to navigate and take away his valuable time of tracking down his own daughter.

Chase picked up the passport-sized photo from the dash, gave it a kiss and drove off into the night rain.

5

ANGEL BLOOD
JO HART

"How may I help you?" I ask, a bright smile plastered across my face. It's part of my job description to look perky. Well, not literally part of my job description, but when you work in retail it's kind of expected. The man, tall, blonde and in his twenties, looks distinctly out of his comfort zone in the lingerie department. Probably buying something for his girlfriend, I think, the usual story. He looks down at me with piercing blue eyes.

"Are you Amanda Bennett?" he asks. His voice is deep, a rumble erupting from his chest.

I nod.

"Can I meet with you when you've finished here?"

"May I ask why?" Usually I'm not one to question the invitation of a tall handsome man, especially since I get so few, but I don't know this guy from a bar of soap and I'm not stupid.

"Sorry," he says, flashing a brilliant smile and

showing off his even white teeth, "I forgot to introduce myself. My name is Ethan Glassey. I believe your life may be in danger."

Really, that's the best pick-up line he has. I can play along. "Are you a cop?"

"No, not exactly. More like Secret Service."

I wasn't aware we even had a Secret Service in our country. Isn't the Secret Service American or British?

"And what makes you think my life is in danger?" I ask. I can't imagine why anyone would think a lingerie store clerk would be worthy of assassination, or why the Secret Service would care.

"I'd rather we speak about this somewhere more private," he intones, looking over his shoulder at the group of women huddled around the bikini rack.

"I get off in twenty minutes."

I'll admit it, I'm curious to know what this guy is all about. The way his eyes keep darting around as if we're being watched seems genuine, not exaggerated the way I would expect if the guy was trying a pick up line. I'm no idiot though. I consider the best place to meet with him. I need somewhere relatively secluded, but somewhere still public and visible in case this guy tries
to pull something.

"I'll meet you at the Sushi Bar by the escalator," I say. "It's usually pretty deserted at this time of day." He nods and I turn my attention to the women looking at bikinis, my bright smile plastered back on my face.

He's sitting in a booth in the back corner of Sushi

Bar when I arrive. I grab a Coke at the counter and make my way to the booth to join him.

"So what's the deal?" I ask, cracking the lid off my Coke. It makes a hiss as the seal breaks.

Ethan scans the room. We're the only customers, if my bottle of Coke gives us the privilege of being called customers that is, and the girl at the counter is texting on her phone.

"What I'm about to tell you may be difficult for you to believe, but you must know it is the truth and it is vital you hear me out." Ethan's face is straight and serious.

"Okay. I'll listen"

"You've heard of fairies, right?"

"Sure, who hasn't."

"What you may not know is that fairies are born from the union of an angel and a human."

"Right. And what have fantasy creatures got to do with me being in danger?"

"It's not fantasy." His blue eyes bore into my own brown ones with fierce intensity. "You need to understand fairies are very real. You are one."

"Excuse me." I look at him with a raised eyebrow. This guy must be on drugs or something. "I think if I was a fairy I would know about it."

"Trust me, you're a fairy."

"And you know this how?"

He scans the room again and leans in closer. I can smell his musky aftershave and I get a little shiver.

"My mentor told me before he was murdered."

"Your mentor?"

"David Renard. He was an angel. He was also your father."

My mum has always been open with me about getting pregnant after a one-night-stand. But my dad an angel? Does he really expect me to believe that?

"You say this David Renard was your mentor, does that mean..."

"I'm an angel too." With another glance at the girl behind the counter (she is still engrossed with her phone), Ethan holds out his hand with his palm facing up. It glows bright white. Just as quickly it returns to normal. "Do you believe me now?"

I nod, then I realise my mouth is gaping open and I quickly snap it closed again.

"So how did David die?"

"A demon killed him. David had a unique power among the angels, he possessed the power of persuasion. He could use this power to persuade humans to do as he wished. Of course being an angel he used it strictly for helping others. He could persuade someone to put down a knife instead of using it to kill his girlfriend, for instance. The demon who killed David wanted to steal this power."

"Did he get it? When he killed David, did the demon steal his power?" I can just imagine what a demon would do with that kind of power, not that I even thought demons were real until now, but if demons are as evil as I think they must be...

"No, he didn't get David's power," replies Ethan.

"Thank goodness. For a demon to steal an angel's power he must kill the angel and drink the angel's blood."

"Eww. So he didn't get to drink David's blood?"

"He did, but it had no effect."

"Why?"

"If an angel's bloodline has been passed on, drinking the blood will not allow the power to manifest inside the demon. Because David's blood lives on in you his blood will have no effect on the demon until you too are dead."

"So this demon wants to kill me?"

"Yes. That's why I'm here. It's my job to protect you."

I take a swig from my Coke, holding the bottle with both hands to stop them shaking.

"Let me get this straight, a demon wants to kill me so he can drink my father's blood and have the power to persuade humans to do whatever he wants?"

Ethan nods. I shudder. A sick feeling forms in my stomach.

"What does this demon look like? Does he look human like you?"

"Yes, he can look like a human just as I can. He has dark hair and green eyes. He's a little shorter than me. His name is Liam Mayfair."

"What am I supposed to do? Do I need to go into hiding or something?"

"Hiding won't help, he'll be able to track you now that he's tasted David's blood. I'll stay with you, I can fight him if he tries to get near you."

"Okay," I agree. There could be worse things than having an extremely handsome body guard come home with me.

I can't remember the last time I had a man inside my house. Actually I can. It was Max Peters from the men's department after we had too much to drink at a work function a couple of months back, but I've been trying to forget that incident.

Ethan gazes around my living room as he comes in, his shoulders are nearly as broad as the doorway. I'm glad I did a load of laundry yesterday and for once there aren't clothes strewn over the couch and chairs (I have a tendency to leave my clothes where I take them off. It's a bad habit my mother abhors). My heart beats a little faster now that Ethan and I are completely alone together inside my house.

"Sorry, I've only got sandwiches for dinner," I say as I head into the kitchen, "My shopping day is tomorrow and I wasn't expecting company."

"That's fine," he calls from the living room.

I rummage through the pantry for bread and spreads. "Peanut butter okay?"

"My favourite," he says, his breath warm on the back of my neck. I didn't even hear him come into the kitchen.

I turn around and face his broad chest. I breathe in his musky aftershave and get a pleasant tingle throughout my body.

"Need any help?" he asks.

"No, I've got it under control," I reply. I can feel my cheeks flush red as I sidestep around him. Even though my eyes are focused on spreading the peanut butter, I can feel him looking at me.

"So I'm a fairy," I say to break the silence, and to deflect his attention from my hands fumbling with the knife. "Do I have special powers?"

"Not exactly," he replies. "You have an essence."

"An essence?" I was hoping for a magic wand or something.

"It's like an inner light, a positive force that affects those around you. You can bring a smile to people's faces just by being near them."

"Hmm." A magic wand would be cooler.

"You're beautiful you know," he says as I finish slathering the peanut butter onto the last slice of bread.

"Yeah right," I reply. I'm still in my orange pin-striped work shirt, which clashes horribly with my red hair.

"You are." He puts a long finger under my chin and gently turns my head to face him.

He looks down at me with his intense blue eyes. Butterflies flutter about in my stomach and my hormones race. He leans down and places his lips on mine. The kiss starts out gentle, his lips brushing softly against my own. Then the kiss becomes harder, more urgent. I clasp my hands around his neck and curl my fingers in his blonde hair. His hands reach around my waist and draw my body closer to his. His tongue flicks at my lips to part them, then probes deeply in my
mouth.

"Sorry," he says as he pulls away. "It's just your lips looked so sweet and soft."

I mumble incoherently in response and my cheeks grow hot. In fact, my cheeks aren't the only part of me left feeling warm after that kiss.

"Umm, why don't you grab the sandwiches and take them into the living room. I need to get out of my work clothes. I'll be back in a sec."

"Don't be long," he says, and I swear his voice is huskier than before.

I try to calm my pulse rate as I climb the stairs to my bedroom. Are all guardian angels like this? Just thinking about his mouth on mine and my body pressed against his sends my heart racing again. Breathe, Amanda, breathe.

I strip off my work clothes, throwing them in a crumpled heap on the floor. I look in the mirror and suck in my stomach. Maybe I should change into some sexier underwear too, just in case. I strip off my grey sports bra and floral undies and search the back of my underwear drawer for the white lacy lingerie set I bought on clearance at the store where I work. I would have bought it just for the clearance price, but I got my employee discount on top of that. I think I've only ever worn it once.

I grab out my sexy black dress, the one with the plunging neckline, and hold it up in front of myself. It would probably look like I'm trying too hard. I don't want to look desperate. I settle upon a denim skirt and white t-shirt. My hair cascades over my shoulders as I pull the hair clasp out. Turning my head side to side I decide it looks okay.

As I turn to head out my bedroom door I catch a glimpse of a person climbing in through my window. My mouth opens to scream, but he appears behind me in a flash. He puts his hand over my mouth with one hand and pins my arms with his other arm by wrapping it around me from behind. I will Ethan to come upstairs.

Do angels work like that? If I send him thoughts will he receive them?

I can see my attacker's reflection in the mirror. He's tall, though not as tall as Ethan, his hair is dark and falls over one eye. The other eye, the one I can see, is a stunning green. Liam. I fight against his hold and he grips tighter.

"Listen to me," he whispers in my ear.

Yeah right, I think.

"I know Ethan must have told you something to make me seem like the bad guy, but it's all lies. Ethan is the one you need to watch out for."

Like I'm going to trust the guy holding me prisoner over the guy who kisses me and calls me beautiful.

"If you promise not to scream I'll let you go so I can explain. If I really wanted to kill you I could have done it by now, right?"

He has a point. I nod my head and he removes his hand from my mouth and loosens his grip. We both sit down on the edge of my bed.

"I'm not saying I believe you," I tell him, "But you have five minutes to explain what you're doing sneaking into my room before I call Ethan up here."

"I've been trying to find you, to warn you about Ethan." His voice is deep, yet soft, like a melody.

"Ethan told me he's an angel, that I need to watch out for *you*."

"He's lying. I'm the one who is an angel, Ethan's the one who's after you."

"Then why hasn't he tried to kill me already? He's had plenty of time since we've been here."

"Did Ethan tell you about David? About how the only way for a demon to steal David's power is to drink his blood?"

"Yes. He told me you're the one who killed him."

"Ethan killed David. Ethan is after David's power. The only reason he hasn't killed you already is because he would need to check if you really are David's daughter."

"How would he check that? Mum never wrote my father's name on my birth certificate."

"He would need to taste you. Has he tried to kiss you or anything like that?"

I gasp. "Yes. And then I came up here straight after."

I sink my head into my hands. He must be just waiting down there for me to come back so he can kill me. I'm such a sucker.

Liam grabs my hands and I look up at him. I notice he isn't bad looking actually. He has a dimple on one cheek and the way his dark hair flops on the one side is kind of cute. Snap out of it, Amanda! Ethan's waiting downstairs to kill me and here I am thinking how cute Liam is.

"I can look after you," Liam says, looking at me earnestly.

I gulp. My chest feels constricted.

"Amanda? Are you okay in there?" Ethan calls from the other side of the door.

I look at Liam wide-eyed.

"I'm fine," I call back, hoping he doesn't notice the squeak in my voice. "I'm just brushing my hair."

"What should we do?" I ask Liam once I'm sure Ethan has retreated back down the stairs.

He leans forward and kisses me gently on my quivering lips.

"Go down and pretend nothing is wrong. Keep him distracted while I come into the room. I'll come from behind and take him by surprise."

I smooth out my skirt as if it will also smooth my nerves as I enter the room. I expect to see Ethan standing there with a knife to greet me (do demons even need to use knives?). He's not standing at all, he's sitting on my brown suede couch munching on a peanut butter sandwich. He's even poured two glasses of
lemonade.

I sit down beside him and pick up a sandwich. He shoots me one of his even white smiles.

"You make a ripper peanut butter sandwich," he says. I laugh.

But I'm confused. Ethan doesn't seem like a killer or a demon. He's sweet and charming. Maybe demons appear that way on purpose. I know Liam is preparing to attack any moment, and I need to know for sure which one is the demon.

"How do I know you are who you say you are?" I ask.

He swallows his mouthful before answering. "That I'm an angel? That David was my mentor?"

I nod.

"You believed me before, what changed?"

"I've just had time to think about it, that's all. I realised you showed me no proof." I wasn't about to tell him about Liam.

"What about at the Sushi Bar? I showed you my power."

"How do I know you're not a demon?"

Ethan opened his mouth to answer, then took a deep breath in through his nose.

"Liam's here. I can smell him. Has he spoken to you? You can't believe a word he says." Ethan grabs my shoulders firmly and looks frantically in my eyes. "You have to trust me."

A blinding white light fills the room. I feel Ethan's hands leave my shoulders. The light subsides and Ethan is sprawled across my now broken coffee table. Sandwiches and lemonade are strewn across the carpet. Ethan scrambles back to his feet, his eyes glaring over my shoulder. I spin around and look. Liam is standing there, his hands glowing white.

"Leave her alone," Liam says, staring right back at Ethan. "I won't let you harm her."

"You're not trying to protect her," Ethan growls. "You're just trying to get me out of the way so you can kill her."

"You really expect her to believe that? I saw you kissing her, Ethan. She knows that's how you check for DNA. She knows you were just checking to see if she's really David's daughter."

I look at Ethan, interested in his answer, hoping to see something in his eyes that gives away his true intent towards me. He remains silent, his mouth slightly open, his eyes showing a hint of fear.

"It's not true," he says, looking at me, but his response is too slow. "I mean it's true that's how a demon checks for DNA, but that's not why I kissed you. I really do like you."

I shake my head, tears prickling at my eyes. I can't even look at him.

"She knows who you truly are, Ethan," says Liam.

"You need to leave."

"No." Ethan's voice is firm.

"Then I must kill you."

Light flashes again. Ethan grunts as it hits his chest. He retaliates, shooting white light in Liam's direction. It misses.

I bite my lip as white light flashes back and forth across my lounge room. The vase of geraniums in the corner smashes into pieces. Feathers erupt from my favourite blue cushion. I want to scream, but I'm frozen to the spot. I don't even know which guy I want to win this fight. Something stirs in me. One of these guys will win and one of these guys wants to kill me. What if the one who wants to kill me is the one who wins? I need to know who is the demon and who is the angel. But how?

They seem to have the same powers. It's not like the demon is shooting red light to give himself away or the angel has feathered wings and a halo. An idea occurs to me.

"I'M NOT DAVID'S DAUGHTER," I shout above the smashing of my glass cabinet.

Both stop and look at me, hands still glowing white.

"I'm not David's daughter," I say again, looking from one to the other. "My father is an accountant in Brisbane, my mother told me."

I hope demons can't sense lies. I keep my face perfectly straight and sincere.

"What do you mean?" Liam asks, staring at me through his bright green eyes. Ethan just frowns with his head cocked to one side.

"I had a paternity test done a few years ago to

prove it. David can't be my father."

"David's your father, Amanda," Liam says slowly, "The paternity test must be mistaken."

Ethan remains quiet.

"How do I kill a demon?" I ask bluntly. My face is stony as I look from one to the other.

They both look taken aback.

"If you throw sea salt," Ethan says, "it will weaken the demon enough to kill it as a mortal. But you must understand an angel can be killed in the same manner."

I understand what he means. If I pick the wrong one, if I pick the angel, he will die the same way a demon will. Of course he could be saying this to deter me from killing the demon, if that demon is him. I don't think either of them really expect me to do anything though, already they're glaring at each other, ignoring me. Their hands are glowing with white intensity. Ethan fires first, hitting Liam in the shoulder and knocking him backwards a step.

They don't notice me slip into the kitchen. I could just leave the house and they'll probably not even realise I'm gone. But what if the demon survives the fight and seeks me out? This will be my best chance to kill the demon, while they're distracted with each other.

I grab the jar of sea salt from the pantry and head back to the lounge room. I'm certain I know who the demon is, but I still feel a flutter in my stomach and a little voice of doubt in my head. I shake the feeling away. Quietly I remove the lid to the jar and grab a handful of salt. Ethan and Liam don't notice me returning to the room. For good measure I duck low behind the couch. Edging along in a squat I get closer to my intended victim.

I see him out of the corner of my eye. He still hasn't seen me. I stand quickly and throw the salt before he can react. His mouth drops in surprise. A flash of light comes from the other side of the room. Liam explodes into a shower of black ash. I look at Ethan and he looks at me. He nods. Liam is gone.

"How did you know it was Liam?" Ethan asks, offering me a glass of lemonade.

The broken items from my lounge room sit in black garbage bags against the wall where Ethan put them to be taken out to the garbage. I switch off the vacuum cleaner to accept the lemonade. There's still a little black residue visible in the fibres of my light brown carpet, but most of it is gone.

"I figured when I said David wasn't my real father whoever was the angel wouldn't argue even if he knew I was wrong, because he wouldn't want to confirm the demon's suspicions. Liam told me straight out that

David was my father, you said nothing."

"Clever." Ethan smiles, showing me those beautiful pearly whites of his.

"Sorry I doubted you," I say.

"You're forgiven. Demons are known to be charming and convincing."

Ethan takes my glass and places it on my sideboard since I no longer have a coffee table. He steps in close to me and looks down into my eyes.

"I suppose you have to go back to heaven, or wherever you live, now?" I say. His closeness is causing that tingle throughout my body again.

"I don't have to go anywhere," he replies. His lips are so close to mine that I can feel his warm breath as he speaks.

My lips quiver and he kisses me. My body melds against his. It feels right.

He pulls away slightly to whisper, "You know it's forbidden for angels to have a relationship with a human."

"Oh." I'm sure he can hear the disappointment in my voice.

"So it's a good thing you're a fairy."

I smile as he brings his mouth back onto mine.

6

FLORA AND JACK
BY MICHAEL WHITE

When they were first married they would go on long picnics in Epping Forest. That was before Nigel and Kate were born. The summers always seemed to be hotter in those days. People said that it was just their memories painting a brighter picture, but they knew otherwise.

Flora Jones laid out the pair of white plates on the table. She placed the lettuce and the tomato slices at the edge of the plates then a slice of ham on the opposite rim. She had been listening to a sad radio play as she prepared the salad. It had been set in the thirties and it had made her remember those sunny summer days and

the ripe tomatoes, red as blood and how the juice trickled down your forearm as you bit into them. Jack had laughed loudly into his own plump fruit as the spray from her tomato hit her in the face. He had wiped her skin with a cotton napkin and kissed her where the juice had landed.

She laid the plates onto a tray and walked through to the lounge where Jack lay in bed. Only his mop of grey hair was visible above the white sheet.

At first he had hated the idea of having the bed moved downstairs. He knew it was practical: He could reach the downstairs toilet and things were easier for Flora, but still he hated the idea.

She woke him with a gentle tap on the shoulder. He opened his eyes and smiled. He had deep blue eyes. They were still clear, but the rest of his face seemed to have died around them.

He tried to sit. The effort was painful to watch.

Flora had seen him slowly fall away from her. Each day, a fresh symptom. Each day, he passed a little further over the horizon.

She helped him up and supported his back with a pillow. She placed the tray on the bed beside her and brought round one of the plates. The food had been cut into small pieces. He opened his mouth as she brought the fork up to his lips. He allowed himself to be fed.

After a few carefully chewed mouthfuls he raised a hand as another forkful of ham and tomato came towards him. He looked into his wife's emerald eyes. His expression was grave. Then he ran his hand, freckled and veined along her cheek. He curled his fingers under her soft chin.

"I think it's nearly time," he said. His voice was almost a whisper now. Once he had been a magnificent baritone.

She knew he meant it. The dread subject had not been broached until this moment. She felt the blood drain from her face. She ran her fingers along his hand.
"I've been dreaming about the woods and the summertime," he said. "Is it still raining out?"
"No, it's stopped now. Sun's come out."
"Oh," he said.
"You not hungry?"
"Not really, love," he said.
She no longer insisted that he eat.
"I'll keep it for later. You warm enough?"
"Fine," he replied.
She put the plate and the tray on a side table and sorted out their bedding. She tucked his thin arms under the sheet and brushed his hair aside with a single, gentle movement. She kissed him on the forehead.
"You sleep a bit," she said.
Before taking the things through to the kitchen she crouched down and turned up the gas fire.
Back in the kitchen the radio was playing some nostalgic music she half recognised. She placed the tray next to the sink and sat down heavily at the table. She looked around the room without really seeing anything.
They had met very young, but their lives together had passed so quickly. Was it really all those years ago that she had stood at the railway station waving Jack goodbye? Little Nigel had stood beside her. She had held his hand so tightly, afraid to lose the one thing
Jack and she had made together. Nigel was only vaguely aware that something was up. She waved and

Nigel waved. Jack's huge hand swept through the air a hundred yards away along the platform.

Jack had looked so gallant, so dashing. They had kissed at the entrance to the station. All around them, other soldiers, wives and girlfriends were making their farewells. Nigel stood beside his parents looking up at

them, trying to figure out what was happening. Jack had picked him up and had made him laugh by tickling him under the arm with his free hand. He had told Nigel to be a good boy, that he had to look after his mum, that he was the man of the house now. Jack had smiled at her and lowered their son to the ground. They looked at each other again. Neither could express the agony they felt.

Jack had picked up his kit and turned towards the waiting train. When he was in the carriage he had lowered the window and leaned out as the train drew away. At that moment she had really believed she would never see him again.

She surveyed the room and then looked out at the patch of green beyond the kitchen window. The sun was shining on the rows of red rooftops. Lower down the hill she could see a middle-aged man cleaning his blue car. He was hosing the bonnet. Water streamed off the end and onto the shiny chrome and the tyres. A little further on, at the base of the hill, two young mothers pushed prams. They were talking, one was smoking. If

she ignored the hum of the radio she could just make out the tap, tap, tap of a neighbour doing some handiwork. It was Sunday and the clouds had all cleared away.

She turned back to the room. Standing up slowly she walked over to the cupboard beside the gas cooker.

It had a yellow door. A painting of a house done by her first great-granddaughter, Sarah, had been pinned Blu-Tacked next to the metal knob. She paused to look at the picture and smiled. Sarah could be a great artist one day. She had her grandfather's eye.

It was six months before Nigel had seen his father again. She and Nigel had been evacuated to Dorset. Jack had been given thirty-six hours leave. He arrived on an army motorbike at dawn. Nigel had been sulky and quiet. Jack had pretended not to be hurt, but she had seen the sadness in his eyes.

That night they made love. It felt as though it had never happened before. She had forgotten how his arms felt. She could hardly recognise the lines in the skin of his neck and the sound of his whispered words.

And then it was all over. Nigel had cried after his father had gone, and they had comforted each other curled up on the sofa.

A year had passed before the dread news came.

The telegram arrived just after breakfast. Nigel had been in a bright mood. He loved the countryside. He had just left for school. She had been sweeping the lounge carpet. The telegram said Jack had been killed in France. The Allies were advancing. She had felt cold.

Nothing had happened until Nigel came home.

There had been no tears, no words, no thoughts. She had sat alone by the lounge window. The wind had blown the clouds across the sun. It was January and it was dark by the time her son returned home.

She opened the cupboard. The bottle of pills stood where she left them beside the tea-caddy. She picked up the bottle and returned to the kitchen table. She knew what the label on the bottle said but she read it again anyway. 'Datolan: one tablet, three times a day before
meals'.

For nearly eighteen months she had believed Jack to be dead, but the War Office had made a mistake. He had been captured near Grenoble. The Germans had been retreating. Conditions in the POW camps had deteriorated; letters had been forbidden.

The war ended. She and Nigel had returned to London. It was late May 1945 and everyone was still in a state of euphoria. She had seen the jubilant crowds and she felt relieved that it had ended. She had lost her husband, but there were millions like her. Now she had to look after her son.

There had been a street party. She had found it difficult to muck in, but she had done it for Nigel's sake. The memory of her last night with Jack still burned in the pit of her stomach.

She had been coming out through the hall, a tray of cakes in her hands. Jack had been standing in the doorway, the early summer sunshine streaming in all around him. The cakes and the tray hit the floor. Even now she could see the walls rushing past her as she dashed forward. His arms were strong. He smelt wonderful.

Two nights after arriving home, Jack announced

that they were going out, uptown for a celebratory meal, just the two of them.

They had wine. Jack order chicken and she had lamb. It was the best meal they had ever had. They talked and talked. It was warm and they ate outside on the balcony of the restaurant and looked out over bomb-shattered London. She pointed out the missing landmarks where the doodlebugs had done their worst.

St Paul's was mostly unscathed, but it stood like a sad mother hen that had lost all her chicks to the wicked fox.

That night was one of the happiest of her life. She felt safe again. Jack, her darling Jack had survived. She had survived and their child, their son, Nigel had survived. Providence had been on their side, and she was so grateful, she felt humbled by it. The coffee had been ersatz but it hardly mattered. She had everything she wanted.

"Jack, I want us to make a promise," she had said. She felt light-headed but never more sure of what she wanted to express.

"What sort of promise, love?" Jack had asked.

"Oh, you'll think I'm being silly."

"No, go on."

How shy she had felt. She had never been shy with Jack before. He looked into her eyes.

"Okay," she had said at last. "I want us to promise that if we live until we're old that we'll die together."

He had look surprised. "Steady on, Flo. Why be so morbid?" he had said.

"No I mean it, Jack." She had fixed him with an insistent stare, suddenly confident.

She could see his face now. He had looked tired, but, oh, so handsome. At that moment, she had adored his every fiber. He and Nigel were her world. "I know you might think I'm being daft, but I love you so much.

I want us to take an oath. I want us to swear that, one day, when we're very old, if one of us is about to die, the other will put us both to sleep. I want us to die together. Will you swear it, Jack. Will you?"

Jack had looked frightened for an instant. He had taken a sip of coffee before returning her earnest gaze.

"Of course I swear," he had said at last.

She had grabbed his hand. "No, I want us to swear it together, now."

Jack had looked so embarrassed, the poor darling. He peered around the room. No one had been looking their way.

"Well if you don't want to…" she had begun, hurt.

"No, no," he had said quickly. "Of course…what shall we swear?" He had regained his composure.

She had told him and they had sworn it together hunched close over the candle flame.

Now, so many years later, that day had arrived. She was terrified.

She knew, as she had known then, that she could not live without Jack. Nothing had changed during those years. Of course, there had been difficult times.

Nine months after that heavenly night, Kate was born. They had so little money that sometimes she really thought they would go under. But things always worked out in the end. Jack had re-started his building business.

There were plenty of people needing work done, but there was so little money to pay for it. Mother had helped with the children and she had found a job at a local shoe factory.

She read again the instructions on the side of the bottle.

It was easy for Jack, he had faith.

She had gone along with his beliefs. She had gone with him to church. She had listened to his ideas, but she could not believe. It was easy for Jack. He was sure of the future, sure of an Afterlife. She saw nothing but a void.

Of course, she still felt the same way she had that night in 1945. She didn't want to live without Jack. It was just that she knew that this was it, the end. Jack was happy, happy inside. He knew they would always be together.

Ironic really, she thought. How strange that blanched expression on dear Jack's face when she had suggested her oath. And now here she was, the one in control. She was the one left with the monumental decision; she, the one lost.

There could be only darkness. Afterwards that is. Darkness and nothingness. 'What would nothingness be like?' she thought, not for the first time. 'When I go to sleep, I feel nothing, I know nothing of the world. But all the same, it goes on without me. I wonder if I'll dream afterwards?'

Suddenly she felt a strange lightness, a sudden sense of freedom. For the first time in her life she really was free. In this terrible moment, when all seemed lost, she felt a wonderful sense of liberation. The family no longer needed her. She had not been needed for a long time. Nigel and Kate had both married and their children had had children of their own. She and Jack had six grandchildren and two great-grandchildren. She was free.

Before lunch she had been looking through a set of old photograph albums. They lay there now where she had left them. She dragged the top one towards her.

There had been the holiday in Scarborough when Nigel had caught a crab and chased Kate with it. She looked tiny.

Jack and she had gone to Paris in 1950. He had worn his wedding suit. It still fitted him. The Eiffel Tower all lit up, the Seine glistening in the moonlight. He had bought her flowers. A maître d' had presented them after coffee at a restaurant in Montparnasse.

Nigel's graduation. He had Jack's fine cheekbones and her chin. Kate's wedding day. Her first baby. Postcards

from Nigel in America. Regent's Park with Nigel's first wife in 1965. Such strange clothes. And the hairstyles…

She closed the album and crossed her palms over the cover. Jack was the only one who needed her. And he was all she needed now.

They had done well, but all good things had to end sometime. She felt calm as she unscrewed the top of the small, brown bottle. She emptied the contents onto the table and counted the small green tablets. There were twenty-two.

She stood up and walked over to the sink, filled the kettle with water and flicked it on.

She never wanted to be a burden. Nigel and

Kate had been angels. Each had offered their home for the time when neither she nor Jack could cope. When Jack had fallen ill the kids had offered their help again.

They were good children.

She felt fine. She could manage. I probably have a few years left in me, she thought as she stared at the kettle. But there was no life without Jack. She never wanted to be a burden to anyone, not even her children.

That would be a living death. No, this was the best way.

If only…

From the drawer beneath the sink she pulled out a rolling pin. Then, from the cupboard beside the refrigerator she fished out a sheet of greaseproof paper.

She placed the paper on the table, scooped up the pills and let them fall from her palm. Folding the paper into four she rolled the cylinder of wood over it a dozen times bearing her weight down onto the twenty-two tablets of Datolan.

When the kettle had boiled she poured the water onto the four teabags in the best china pot to make a strong brew. Opening the greaseproof paper she looked with satisfaction at her handy-work. The pills were completely powdered. She took a knife from the drawer and divided the pile into two.

The Datolan made two tiny mounds in the bottom of each teacup. She added milk and a spoonful of sugar to each. The tea was ready. She placed the strainer on the rim of the first cup and poured the hot liquid over the mixture. She repeated the process with the second cup then stirred them both. She sat back in her chair and stared at the two cups.

She tried to remember a time when she had believed. It was difficult.

It had been about six months after Jack had gone. Nigel and she were in Dorset by then. The skies were full of fighter planes. There had been three days of dogfights. Along with everyone else, she had known instinctively that her fate lay in the balance. Those few men overhead would determine the future.

It had been near dusk on the third day when the German plane came down in the field next to the village pub. It had screamed over the rooftops, its tail aflame.

Somehow, the pilot was managing to keep it level. He brought the nose up from a crash dive. He had guided the plane into the field. It had landed with a bump and had disappeared into the trees at the far end, away from the village.

She was the first to arrive at the scene. The pilot was unconscious. He was slumped forward over the joystick. She had given no thought to the danger and had tried to unbuckle him. Peter Southgate, the landlord of the pub had got there a few minutes later. By then the pilot had died. A stream of crimson liquid had run down between his open eyes.

"Thank God the filthy bugger's dead," Southgate had said. He had laughed at the man's pain, sneered at his death. "The only good German, what…?"

That night she had a dream about the dead pilot. She tried to picture his wife, his children, the pain they would feel. She had seen his wallet. Two blond boys.

His wife had a pretty face. In the dark she could see again Southgate's glee. From that moment she had begun to lose all faith in humanity. She realised then that you had to have faith in human beings to have faith in God.

The radio brought her back. She smiled at the familiar melody of *Moonlight Serenade*.

It was fear of the abyss. Quite a natural thing, really, she thought. There would be nothing after, after she had done it. There could be nothing. She couldn't believe in heaven. There was no God, at least not a God who looked after each human life. That was impossible.

"I'm just not that important," she said aloud. "I've been very lucky. I've had a wonderful life. I married the best man in the world. I have given birth to beautiful children and we have all been happy. To expect anything more would be greedy. I know that after today there will be nothing, but I've had it all already."

She stood up and walked over to the window. She looked out across the housing estate. Down the hill, the middle-aged man was still cleaning his blue car. The mothers had gone, but there would be others walking that way soon, and more after them. She pulled the red blind down to cover the view. The room was suddenly thrown into gloom. She walked back to the table. She took down the best tray from the shelf above the table and placed the cups of tea in the center.

Near the sink there stood a tall, thin vase. A single red rose leaned towards her. Kate had turned up with it the day before. She took it from the vase and laid it next to the cups. Then, as an afterthought, she reopened the photo album and turned the pages. Eventually she found the picture she had been looking for. It had been

taken at the street party, within an hour of Jack's return from the dead, She stared at it for a long time. They had stood arm in arm. Jack was in his army uniform. The brass buttons on his jacket sparkled in the sunshine. Behind the two of them, bunting, smiling faces and trestle tables covered with white cloths, the Union Jack draped over a doorway. Her dress had blown tight about her thighs.

She pulled the picture away from the page and placed it beside the teacups.

Back in the lounge, Jack lay asleep where she had left him. She sat down beside the bed and placed the two cups on the bedside table. She looked at her husband. Asleep, he was a world away from her. But she knew that she could wake him and they could talk.

Later, they would both enter the darkness, but each a different darkness. They would separate at last. Jack believed they would be together in a beautiful heaven where there was no pain, only togetherness and peace. It was good he thought that. She was glad he believed.

She looked at Jack's grey face and his grey hair. One day, many years before, she had looked at that same face as he had said: "I do." He had been so young.

The future had lain before them. He had worn his only suit and a silver tie. A red rose in his lapel. His hair had been black and very thick, his eyes bright

and clear. He had been very nervous and so adorable.
'Why was time so cruel?'

She kissed his forehead. He opened his eyes.

"I've made us some tea," she said.

She smiled down at him. "Can I get in beside you?"

He looked at her and his cheeks appeared to sink under his eyes. He smiled weakly and steeled himself for the pain of sitting up. She helped him again and then walked round the end of the bed. She placed her tea on a cabinet her side of the bed and kicked off her slippers.

She puffed up the pillows and slid under the covers. She showed Jack the photo. They both smiled.

"You're more beautiful now," he said.

She laughed. "And I love you even more."

She picked up the rose. They each smelt it.

"Roses are still my favourite flower," he said.

"Mine too. Kate brought it over."

They sat together, their free hands entwined tightly under the heaped blankets.

"You know, when I'm better," Jack said suddenly. "We ought to have the kids over. Have a little party to celebrate. What do you think?" There was a brightness in his voice she had not heard for a long time.

"Wonderful," she said. "I could bake a cake. That Thomas gets bigger every day. He loves my currant cake."

"And we should see Arthur and Gladys again. It's been years." She nodded in agreement, knowing they had both died during the nineties.

When the cups were empty, she took his and put

them on her beside cabinet.

"How was that?" she asked.

"You've always made lovely tea, Flo. Always been a wonderful wife."

"I've tried my best," she said.

Suddenly there was no sadness. She had lived so many happy years with the man she loved. What more could she ask for? It was done, she was content.

"Hold me," Jack said. "I feel a bit shivery."

She pulled the covers up under their chins and he nuzzled into her shoulder. She kissed the top of his head and held him close. She looked at the ceiling and then at the orange patterned curtains past the end of the bed. She could hear Jack's heart beat and she could feel his warmth.'

7

MY PLACE
BY BELINDA DORIO

The heat bore down on me like a smothering blanket I couldn't kick off, however frantically I tried. Even when the sun went to sleep and the moon rose, the summer nights were stifling hot in outback Victoria. I tried to block out the strangled cat noise that emanated from the house as I hurried down the back steps of the
porch before picking up into a run, afraid Mum would follow me out of the house, whirling her vodka bottle or something worse.
My breath came out in short hot pants as I sent a silent prayer up to God, if he happened to be listening or even existed, to thank him for my secluded upbringing as my boots whipped through the knee high dry grass of the side paddock. Our property was the perfect escape from the chaos and violence that my mother so gladly provided me. I slowed my pace as I shot restless glances back at the house, the lights

shining out of the small windows peacefully and the bull nose porch promising false safety and warmth. My pace slowed as her shrieks died in the night air and I couldn't see the traitor house that was my 'home'. I brushed the leaves of a low-hanging gum tree branch out of the way and stepped into my secret hiding place.

I took a deep breath in through my nose and my eyes closed in bliss as a refreshingly cold wash of relief flushed out from my stomach, the instant feeling of calm always eased through my bones when I stepped through the line of trees that circled the small clearing, almost like how you can feel an ice cold drink slide down your throat and into your stomach on a scorching
hot day.

The grass of my place is dry and itchy and feels a little like lying on a bed of soft nails as I ease down in the knee high grass and the rest of the world fades away as I lay encased amongst it. The night smells like nothing else in the world; smooth, crisp and clean like freshly washed linen. I breathed a sigh of relief as I rested my head on my hands and my heart lurched in
my chest as I closed my eyes. I knew I had to leave, had to get away from my destructive mother - but every time I tried, I was overwhelmed with such a physical
weight of guilt that I always chose to stay, hoping that tomorrow she wouldn't be swigging from a bottle. I looked up at the slither of moon that hung recklessly in the sky, only the faint outline of the true size of its beauty visible in the darkness. I felt my mouth tug

into a jaded smile as I stared up at a solitary star that punctured the night and thought how alike that star and

I were - so alone. I craned my neck all the way back to see if I could spot any more stars and froze as I noticed the dark shape of a person standing at the edge of my clearing.

Instantly I shrank back into my hiding place, reassuring myself that mum wouldn't be able to see me concealed amongst the grass. Why hadn't I heard her approach?

Surely she would have made a ruckus in her drunken stupor, thundering through the grass and trees, disturbing my beautiful night? I rolled onto my stomach as quietly as I could, straining my ears for the sound of my discovery, but I only heard the crackling of the dried grass beneath me and my staggered breathing. I bent my elbows slightly and pushed my toes to the

ground, ready to spring up and dart away like a frightened rabbit if she should find me. My eyes were unfocused, yet glued on the stalks of wispy brown grass in front of me as they swayed from side to side in the moonlight.

"Hello? Is anyone there?" a soft voice asked.

I glanced up at the voice, and saw a small child at the edge of my trees as I felt my muscles loosen from their tense state.

"What do you want, kid?" My voice was dispassionate as I lay back down.

The small girl edged closer. She must have only been about eight years old. *What is she doing out this late at night?*

"I'm sorry, I sometimes come here… to get away"
Her dirty blonde hair stuck to her face in long strands.
A derogative snort came out of my throat seemingly
of its own accord and I watched long enough to see
the hurt flit through the girl's dark eyes. Guilt tried to
stab at my heart but I pushed the familiar feeling
away. *She must live at one of the houses nearby.*
"And what would you know of needing to get
away?" My laughter filled the hot night air. "Get out.
This is my place. My only place. Get out." I closed
my eyes and didn't open them again until I heard the
small girl slowly wade through the grass the way
she'd come.
I stared up at my solitary star and felt a hot tear
drop down my cheek and hated myself for it. *Do you
really exist if no one in the world loves you?*
Shards of too-bright light stabbed at my closed
eyelids, making my sight turn a reddish pink. I sat up
groggily, picking straw from my hair as I stretched
my protesting limbs and tried to gulp down the humid
morning air. I glared up at the relentless ball of fire in
the sky, it always signaled the time when I would go
back to mum. Guilt pulled at me as if there were a
string tied around my heart and it would tug and tug
until I followed it back to her, despite her dangerous
mood swings and addiction to the bottle.
I peeled myself from the grass, and smiled at the
indent my body left amongst it. I walked slowly, my
feet trailing behind me unwillingly as the house
loomed into view, the old cattle fences hanging old
and rusted,
like broken bones morbidly circling the backyard.
The soft light of morning filtered through the canopy

of gum trees that surrounded our small weather board house as I climbed up the worn verandah, trailing my hand along the peeling paint on the hand rail. The house didn't always look like this, with its missing planks, peeling paint, mismatched window sills and crooked door. I lingered at the entrance after wrenching the rusted fly wire door aside with some effort,

remembering what life was like not that long ago, before Dad went away.

He would take me, my brother and sister on bike rides around town, laughing and joking before returning to mum who would be waiting peacefully whilst pottering in the garden. I remembered the way the sunshine played in their hair, the way it lit up their faces as if they were angels. And I remembered, more vividly

than anything – the soft smile and glow in my mother's eyes as she welcomed us home. But that was long ago now and my elder siblings had fled, leaving me to deal with a person I could barely call a mother. I sighed and pushed open the door, gagging at the rancid smell that immediately sought out my nose. Oh God, mum. I moved cautiously to the lounge, afraid that she might still be conscious, worried that she might not be. I felt as if I was wading through thick sticky syrup as I got closer and closer to the couch where I could see her leg sticking out from behind it at an odd angle, the air was too thick, too hot to breath. It was then I heard the gurgling sound.

"Mum!" I yelled as I rushed over to her.

She lay on her back, her body slightly convulsing, with a sickly yellow liquid dribbling from her mouth and down her cheek as she suffocated on her own vomit.

A string of curses left my mouth as I fluttered around her, not knowing how to start.

Then I felt myself leave, like I often did. My mind took a back seat as my body took control, my breathing returning to a slow, calm rhythm. My hands stopped shaking and I grabbed hold of my mother sturdily as I rolled her onto her side, not flinching when vomit spilled out onto my lap. I couldn't smell, couldn't feel, and could only see. Complete detachment; it was utter bliss. I inserted two fingers into her mouth and dug out the chunks. Some part of my mind noted the disgusting feel of her tongue, but was quickly pushed back away into that small dark place inside me. And when she started to cough, I sighed in relief and my heart continued its broken beat in the cage of my chest.

"Mum?" She tried to sit up as she raised her blurry eyes to mine.

"What are you lookin' at?" She slurred as she struggled back onto the couch, reaching for her bottle of vodka on the coffee table. She murmured an obscenity when she realised it was empty, before she threw it against the wall. Pieces of glass rained onto the floor.

I'll have to clean that up later.

I turned from her before her rage could be directed back at me, but a little too late.

"Yeah run away you scared little rabbit, useless child." And I heard the click of her lighter igniting another cigarette. I didn't turn when I answered her. "I am not a child anymore, mum" *and I haven't been for years.*

"Sure, sure" She muttered then showered off the insides of her stomach as I walked down the hallway to the bathroom.

I pulled on my old work uniform; second hand, of course. The jumper had holes in the elbows, but I stopped worrying about what I looked like a long time ago. Somehow I didn't think the people at the petrol station cared much. I would often mourn my lack of education when I re-read a dog-eared text book from year ten. I would trace the illustrations of the history pages with my finger or my read a piece of poetry aloud in perfect rhythm. But it had been years since I had

been in school, Mum had demanded that I start working as soon as possible to help support myself - to free up more money for booze, I'm sure.

I checked on mum unwillingly before I left, her frail body draped over the couch, her eyes closed - unconscious again, still caked in her vomit.

I tried not to think about all my old friends who had gone to University last year, all of those faces who had long forgotten me and forced smiles and greetings when they came to fill up their cars at the petrol station.

I snuck out the door and rushed to my car, a 1985 green corolla, the door creaking as I open it. I slank into the worn seats thankfully. I sighed when I inhaled the 'new car' smell of my air freshener, and I couldn't help but smile ruefully at the irony. The old girl started on the first go. At least fate had spared me car troubles.

The trip to work was too quick, and I wound down my window all the way, enjoying the sunny day as my still-damp hair billows out the window. I pulled up at the petrol station in a wave of red dust and heard my boots crunch on the gravel as I step out of the car, sighing as I leant back against my trusty green beast. The heat of the metal seared my back in a way that was somehow comforting.

Sometimes I felt like I was stuck in a bubble, and that no one else saw the world the way I did. Or maybe it was that I was on the other side of a glass wall, pounding on it and begging to be let in, but no one ever heard me. I could hear the chime of the petrol station door as people rushed in and out, always on their way somewhere and always moving. Why don't people slow down? I wonder if they knew what it was like to just be,

to be in one place and to be still. The thought made my heart yearn for my secluded place in the side paddock, but I pushed the thought away.

The day passed slowly, people coming in and out the door all wearing the same expression, all struggling with the heat as sweat dotted their brows and ran slowly down their necks, all with varying degrees of body odor wafting off their hot bodies.

But when the door chimed at around lunch time my eyes widened as she came in, dragged by a large man wearing a flannelette shirt and a trucker hat - so stereotypical it made me want to laugh. I felt my heart still as I took in the angle at which he was holding her frail wrist, and the screams that tore from her throat.

So familiar I could almost feel the hand on my wrist, the painful twist as the bones began to protest the pressure, the desperation as the one person who is supposed to protect you harms you in the most awful way. Heat boiled in my chest and I felt my fists clench as the man came to the counter; shoving the small girl into a stand
of chips and wiping the back of his hand across his nose. She looked different under the harsh lights, frailer, more pathetic.

"Number 5" he grunted as he threw a $20 note at me. Each of my muscles locked into place and I lifted my eyes slowly from his money lying on the counter into his beady brown eyes. That frantic look loomed beyond the surface of his eyes, the look my own mother had in hers. The little girl had begun sobbing but had picked herself up, cradling her wrist.

"Get out" I said in a low voice I barely recognised. The man paused for a moment, his eyes still intent on me.

"Excuse me?" he laughed and the sound sent shivers down my spine as he placed his large hands on the counter in what he probably thought was a threatening gesture.

I smiled.

"Leave your daughter here and get the hell out before I call the police"

"And who do you think you are?" Spittle flew from his lips and I could smell cheap bourbon on his breath.

His daughter edged towards the back of the store, where a door led to the staff room.

I shrugged and took a seat, placing my boots atop the counter, my hands behind my head.

He leaned across the counter to grab me.

"I wouldn't do that if I were you" I said, gesturing towards the surveillance camera that blinked its red light above us.

"Wouldn't want to go back to jail, would you?" I asked with another smile on my face as I took in the doves tattooed on his hands. He was someone who knew what the inside of a cell looked like. I remembered my uncle showing me his once as he smiled rotting teeth at me, amused at my shock.

The large man faltered for a moment and I saw something move behind those grotesque eyes. Fear? Surely not.

"Whatever, she's a stupid little tramp anyway. She can find her own way home" he pouted and stormed out without a backwards glance for his daughter. I felt my lip curl in disgust.

I found the girl hiding out the back, huddled behind some boxes with her head in her hands. Her nails were chipped and obviously bitten, with dirt caked under them. Her blonde hair was mangy and hung in clumps.

Tears streaked her face. I wondered how long it had been since she bathed.

Guilt stabbed me harder than anything I had ever felt and I staggered under the harshness of it. I remembered the way I had laughed at the little girls plea to stay and share my hiding place.

I bent down, my hands hovering uncertainly above her.

"It's ok" I said, in what I hoped was a soothing

tone.

She glanced up. "He's coming isn't he?" Her eyes showed too much white around her blue irises.

"No, I sent him away" I reached out a hand for her and after a moment she placed her little hand in mine as dark uncertainty floated behind those eyes. I'd never thought of myself as maternal, but looking down at this poor child I felt an overwhelming urge to protect her.

"What's your name, sweetie?"

"Millie" she said in her small voice and I rewarded her with a smile.

"I'm Sarah, Millie, and I think you and I need to get away from this place - don't you think?"

Another moment of hesitation. "I'd like that" said Millie.

The dry grass stabbed at my back through my thin shirt but the sensation only reminded me that I was safe in my hiding place and I breathed a sigh of relief. Millie lay near me somewhere, though I couldn't see her through the tall grass that separated us like a sheet drawn in a changing room. My mind whirled at what I was going to do with the girl. Although I had acted brave in front of her father, I was afraid he was going to come back for me and I shuddered as I remembered his beady brown eyes. I thought of my mother pacing in the house in one of her drunken states, wondering where I was and I forced myself not to go and check on her. I rubbed my hand across the grass and my anxiety lessened but didn't completely abate, the time for action was now. I had to do something – but what?

I didn't sleep much that night, barely at all actually as I prepared everything I needed. And when the sun started rising in strips of pink and blue I waited awhile before waking Millie, a piece of poetry floating in my mind *'I'll tell you how the sun rose, one ribbon at a time..'*

She lay there huddled in the grass sound asleep, mangy blonde hair wrapped around her neck as her eyelids fluttered spasmodically; I vaguely wondered what she dreamed of as I shook her gently. This wasn't the place for a child, huddled amongst the dry grass under the hot sun.

When Millie stirred awake I knew I would never forget the wariness in those little blue eyes, the mistrust that loomed beneath the cornfield blue surface even when she smiled and said good morning. Millie had shown me that sometimes change needs to happen and that you sometimes need to leave those toxic people in your life behind before their poison leaks into you.

"Morning, sweetie" my lips pulled into a smile I hoped was reassuring, "Ready to get going?" I asked. She didn't ask where I was taking her, but just bobbed her little head and grabbed my hand. Her hand was so frail inside mine and I found myself patting it idly as we walked from our clearing.

Today I stopped at the old cattle fence and pressed my hand to the splintering timber, part of me hoping that I would never forget what it felt like to be home, part of me hoping I would never remember. My gaze went to the house, that 'home' that always lured me back and I felt tears prick at my eyes.

I'd been avoiding leaving, even though my bags

had been packed for months and my bank account continued to swell with my careful saving.

"You 'kay?" asked Millie in a small voice. Her hand gripped mine tighter and a betraying tear dripped down my face.

"Of course, kiddo. Let's go, shall we?"

I didn't walk under the shade of the gum trees today, didn't hear the protest of the old porch steps as I eased up them. Instead I turned and headed towards that old car of mine with Millie walking beside me. I opened the passenger door for Millie as a blast of hot air wafted out and I saw her glance at the bags I had piled on the back seat but again, she said nothing. The slam of my door seemed especially loud today and I winced in the driver's seat as I gripped the hot steering wheel, my keys jangling as I fumbled to insert them into the ignition. I closed my eyes and took a deep breath before turning the key. I gazed out at my old home, my eyes lingering on that side paddock where I knew my place laid waiting for me and I wondered what my poor mother was doing. But I couldn't think of that anymore. And so, I backed out of the drive and with one last look at the house with the bull nosed verandah I headed into town.

I didn't know how Millie would take being handed over to the police, but she didn't protest, didn't say anything actually, as I explained to an officer with kind eyes what I was doing with an eight year old girl who looked like she hadn't showered in a week. Millie listened carefully and answered any questions directed at her with one word answers and my eyes kept darting to her, waiting for a tear, a crack in her voice, but there was nothing but simple answers and that weariness in her eyes that reminded me of an alley cat that was ready to run scampering down the street at the first sign of danger.

After evaluation, he told me Millie would be taken into foster care and placed with a family. As I hugged her goodbye she whispered 'thank you' into my ear and I sent a prayer up to God, begging him to watch over her. The policeman promised me he would take good care of her and I watched as a social worker took Millie's hand and led her into a room with a promise of a mug of hot chocolate that seemed to light up Millie's eyes, if just for a moment. And then the door closed and she was gone.

As I left the air-conditioned hush of the police station and trudged back to my car I promised myself I would search for Millie again one day. One day when I had a home and a family of my own, someplace far from here. And I knew, without even having to form the thought in my head that I would come back for my mother. One day when I wasn't this lanky nineteen-year-old that worked at a petrol station and slept in the paddock beside her house. One day when I knew who I was, when I knew I could get her the help she needed. I just hope I wouldn't be too late. My hands were clammy and the shirt I slept in last night clung to the wet patch on my back as I wound down my window as far as it could go.

Maybe I'd go someplace where the heat didn't bear down on me like this, where it doesn't feel like I'm suffocating.

I started my car again. I didn't know where I was going. I just hoped it would be somewhere I could breathe a little easier.

8

A BRILLIANT MAN
BY SONALI RAJANAYAGAM

When he was a young man, my father would travel 60 miles for a dance. Premathan Vikramathi rolled into my mother's village in the late afternoon like the cool breeze that blew in from the sea, unsettling the red dust that had hung heavy in the day. One hand lazily at the wheel of his white Daimler, the other drumming the roof in time to the song that was playing in his head, Prem turned to his wingman T.G. and gave a wink. The blast of the car's horn scattered the gulls that had gathered in anticipation of the returning fishing boats.

Laying their mischief aside, children spilled out from verandas and door stoops and ran to the street, hoping for a turn riding on the side board. Prem pulled over in the shade of a giant fig and the kids took turns pushing the horn and winding the windows. Pretty girls in crisp white frocks stayed safely indoors, holding their breath and stealing glances at the circus outside each time the ceiling fan lifted the curtains just so. The servant girls, emboldened by their plight, found excuses to walk by the young men. But having courted their gaze, an easy smile from one of the young men would send them giggling and squealing back to their chores.

Sixty miles for a dance? Who does that? Most nights, I couldn't even be bothered driving to the video store. It had been one of my mother's stories of course.

When I could not understand some slight at the hands of my father, some words unsaid or an empty chair in a sea of eager faces, she would wrap me up in stories of their past. I was never quite sure whether to believe these tales - tales of this strange man in a strange land.

He never spoke of this past. It had been shed just as surely as he had the skin of his homeland. That part I could understand. The country that had pulsed in his veins, that which he could always count on, had turned on him. And he, in a Boeing 707, had turned on it. But

that easy smile of which my mother spoke, that was more foreign to me than the home he had fled.

I hesitated a moment, then knocked quickly at the door. Part of me hoped that he had forgotten. But instantly I felt that familiar guilt - too long, my father's child - so I knocked louder before I could change my mind about the whole thing.

I could hear the fall of his feet, regular, efficient and without deviation. There was a muffled cough and the un-clicking of locks.

"You're late."

Damn. Of course he hadn't forgotten. I held my
tongue, and kissed him awkwardly on each cheek.
"Okay Dad. Let's go."
"Just give me a minute."
He turned to make his way back down the hall.
That would give me time to have a cup of tea. I could
definitely use the caffeine.
"Not too long now Dad. It'll take at least three hours
to get down there."
Dad closed his bedroom door. We did our little dance.
He behind the door, smoking like a teenager. Me in
the kitchen, pretending not to know what he was up
to. He would swipe at the smoke, the smell fading
silently into his bedroom walls. I would pretend not to
notice his coughing. He would pretend he didn't
know that I knew. There was a comforting familiarity
in the deceit.
The kitchen was neat as usual, everything in its place.
Not like when I was a child. Then, the place had been
a constant mess - letters waiting to be opened, bills
waiting to be paid, dishes waiting to be cleaned, life
waiting to be attended to. There had been noise too -
the new single I had bought that week, my sister
turning the television up louder and louder as she sat
closer and closer, and my mother's laugh. Always,
my mother's laugh.
The kettle hummed steadily. The tea bags had been
moved from their usual spot, so Dad must have had a
day off since I last saw him. He'd probably been
ordered to. I'd met Bill, the chief of surgery, at Dad's
work Christmas party last year, and from the way he
was talking I think we both knew that Dad was more
likely to die at the operating table rather than on it.

I scoured the cupboards for the tea bags. Dad's kitchen operates on a Dewey Decimal System of sorts, so once I spied the coffee beans, I knew I was getting close. And there they were, the tea bags filed neatly between the hot chocolate and the green tea. Green tea?

When did he start drinking green tea? It must have been a gift from one of his patients.

Had Irene given gifts to the doctors at the end? Or were gifts only required if everything went well? A kind of KPI for the medical profession.

The funeral would be starting at 11. Why did I offer to do this? A road trip? To Canberra? With my father? Dad didn't even want to go. I should have just kept my big mouth shut. He had said he had back to back surgeries. Still, even I was surprised when he had said he wasn't going. T.G. had been his best man for God's sake. Does nothing touch this man?

The anger rose in my throat as I reached for the kettle. I missed the cup and hot water spilt over onto the bench. My father doesn't believe in sponges. It must be his surgeon's sensibilities - he doesn't use hankies either. Anything that has been in contact with germs is discarded. I reached for the paper towels in the cupboard under the sink but found the garbage bin. Where would they be - with cleaning gear or paper products? I didn't know and I didn't have time to search the catalogue for their whereabouts. In the old days there would have been a stack of bills or yellowed phone messages to use to soak up the mess. I grabbed at a ball of paper that had been thrown into the bin. A torn envelope. I smoothed it out and smiled perversely at the idea of cleaning Dad's benchtop with something from the kitchen bin.

The hot tea worked. I was determined that today would be different. A smoking workaholic doctor who never takes his own advice. That bomb is ticking. I didn't want to be one of those people who lose their parents without ever really knowing who they were.

That is a mid-life crisis that I could do without. I had enough others to keep me occupied right now.

I played with the damp envelope in my hands. I folded it again and again to see how small I could make it. It is a habit that I inherited from my mother. I once heard at school that you can only fold any piece of paper in half seven times. I have found that to be true. I unfolded the envelope and began to fold it the other way.

The sender's name on the envelope caught my eye. T.G. Nawaswaran. The letters were formed in big, friendly loops that were decidedly feminine. The envelope was from St. Stephen's Hospice, Canberra and postmarked three days ago. One of the nurses must have posted it for Uncle T.G. just after he died. I heard Dad close his bedroom door. I crushed the envelope into the palm of my hand as he appeared in the doorway. I felt like a voyeur but I didn't know why.

I pretended not to notice him as I ambled to the sink and took great pains washing my cup. When I was sure he wasn't looking, I quickly tucked the ball of paper back in the bin. But when I turned back, he was staring at me.

"Ready, Thelma?"

He stared at me blankly. "We're taking my car" he said.

"You know I can't drive your car. It's a manual."

"I told you to learn on a manual –"

"Why do you still go on about that?"

"Doesn't matter now. We'll take my car, and I'll drive -"

"You're not driving. The whole point was for me to drive you."

"That's ridiculous. Why can't I drive?"

The truth was that I had thought he would be too emotional to drive. But now I could see that was completely misguided.

"Fine! You drive."

He jiggled the keys in his pocket. He had known all along that he would win that battle. It was an old wound and a hot day, and I blurted out before I could stop myself.

"What did Uncle T.G. say?"

The jiggling stopped.

"What do you mean?"

"The letter he sent you. What did he say?"

"How do you know about that?"

"I saw the envelope."

He shook his head. "Nothing. Come on, let's go."

Nothing? Nothing? A letter from Uncle T.G. on his deathbed, and it said nothing? When would he stop treating me like a five year old?

I waited outside by the kerb while Dad locked up the house, moving methodically from front to back, checking the windows in each room no matter how long they had been unoccupied. Eventually his car emerged and he pulled over to let me in. As we drove past my car, he shook his head. I knew what was coming.

"I don't know why you bought that car."

"Because it's cheap to run and easy to park."

"But it's not Australian. You should have bought an Australian car. Supported the economy."

"You drive a BMW! How is that supporting the local economy?"

"It's different for me now. But when I came to this country, I bought a Holden."

I turned the radio on before I could say something else that I would in time regret.

Three and a half hours of this. My sister had told me this was going to be a waste of time. A fool's mission. He's just not that deep, she'd told me. I'd asked her to join us - it would be just like the old days, after Mum died - the three of us. That had sealed it for her - my sister decided then and there that she wouldn't be joining us. She told me she wouldn't have been able to afford the therapy afterwards. I told her my shrink might give us a family discount - seeing as our problems have a common root. She said she was talking about therapy of the liquid kind.

***

We listened in silence to Radio National until we reached the freeway. The only sign of life in our car was when we shifted uncomfortably during an interview with a sex therapist. Oh yeah. This trip was going great.

Suddenly Dad pulled the car over into a service road. He turned off the engine and reached for the door handle.

"Okay. Get out of the car."

Dad was halfway around to my side of the car before I could pull my thoughts together.

"What are you doing?"

Dad yanked the car door open.

"I'm teaching you how to drive a manual. I should have done it years ago. Come on, get out!"

"What? Now? Here on the freeway?"

"Why not? It's a three hour trip and we haven't got anything else better to do. Come on! Hurry up."

Driving lessons? They'd gone so well the first time around. But as I walked around the front of the car, the December sun warm on my back, I began humming Paul Kelly's "To Her Door". That had been my song that summer - the one that I played over and over. I buckled myself in, school was over for good and I could achieve anything.

"Alright. Adjust your mirrors. ... Here, like this. ... Now, your left foot goes on the clutch. You can't change gears without pressing on the clutch. Try it and see what happens. ... You see? Nothing. ..."

***

"Do you want to swap over again? I think this rain is going to get harder."

"No. I don't need to. I think you've got the hang of it."

Despite myself, the warmth of his praise seeped through my body.

"So when was the last time you saw Uncle T.G.?"

"Don't forget to keep an eye on the tachometer."

Dad turned his head toward the window. "It was the end of October. I went down there as soon as Irene told me."

"How was he when you saw him?"

"As you'd expect. It was just before he went into the hospice. There wasn't anything I could do by then."

I remembered then that he had been away. Neither my sister nor I had heard from him for a while, and we'd argued about who should be the first to call him. We'd played paper, scissors, rock and I had won.

"I can't believe it happened so suddenly."

"It didn't. He'd been seeing an oncologist for nearly a year but he'd decided he wasn't going to fight it." Dad picked at something on the upholstery. "T.G. never told Irene that anything was wrong. If he had, she would have made him do something - she would have found the best specialists, she would have gotten second opinions, she would have asked me to do something. There isn't anything she wouldn't have done for that man. But she only found out when he collapsed on the bus on his way to work. The man had a tumour the size of a melon and he was still sitting on that damn bus like there was nothing wrong. That man never thought about tomorrow. He just never gave a damn."

I listened for a while to the rain on the roof, and I let him listen to the conversations that were replaying in his head, arguments that were too late to have, words that couldn't be taken back.

"Maybe he didn't want his final months to be about the cancer?"

"Well you don't get a choice about that." He began picking at the upholstery again. I could see a dark fleck buried in the fibres. He was working his way around its edge with his nail. "T.G. had a wife and children. If he knew he only had months to live, he owed those last few months to them. It was wrong not to tell them."

"So why didn't he?"

"You'd have to ask him."

"Didn't he tell you in his letter?"

"No."

"Well what did he say then? I mean, in his letter?"

"Nothing." He rubbed harder at the fleck. "What does it matter to you? It was just a letter. Not everything has to mean something."

My fingers tightened on the steering wheel and my foot pressed a little harder on the accelerator.

"Not everything, but some things. Some things should mean something." My pathetic Dr Phil-osophising hung unclaimed in the air and I wanted to reach out and take it back.

"That's the problem with you Jenny. You're always trying to make things more complicated than they are."

I pressed down a little harder still.

"Jenny, you're going too fast."

I pulled out to overtake the semi-trailer in front of us, and the spray from his tyres blinded us for a moment. I felt the car slide for the tinniest fraction of a second before decades of trusty German engineering righted us once more.

He shouted at me to pull over.

When I did, he shoved the door open so hard that it slammed back at first. He pushed it away again and as he got out I saw that the fleck had become a mark. At his worrying fingers, the fleck had bled into the fabric.

***

We drove the rest of the way in silence. Even when we got stuck in traffic for an hour because of an accident near Goulburn. For me, it was time spent reliving past injustices. I had no idea what he was doing with his.

Of course we missed the funeral. By the time we reached Canberra and found the cemetery, all the mourners had gone. Dad pulled over and eventually we found Uncle T.G.'s grave. Two young men in overalls were talking loudly about the cricket while they shoveled fresh dirt into the grave. They stopped and moved away awkwardly as they saw us approaching.

Dad took a handful of the dirt and scattered it into the grave. I left him squatting by its side and wandered off to stretch my legs.

He'd told my mother that she smelled like coconuts, papaya, and rain in the afternoon. That was when she fell in love with him. It wasn't the way his eyes flirted dangerously about her when he thought she wasn't looking. And, despite her teasing, she hadn't fallen in love with him because of the way his cream shirt and trousers looked as crisp and clean as the moment they'd arrived from Marks and Spencer. It was the way he'd noticed every little thing about her.

***

We talked in the car on the way to the wake. Safe topics - my nieces, the new magnolia Dad's gardener had planted, the hymns I would be singing at the Christmas service - played gently between us like water lapping at the shore.
I toyed with the idea of waiting in the car while Dad went to the wake, but I couldn't do that to Irene. She'd been a favourite of mine as a kid. Irene was young and Australian and therefore an instant hit with my sister and me. As a new bride, Irene had been determined to embrace her husband's culture. She had tried the clothing, the food, and the decor. But with little interest, or apparently guidance, on the part of Uncle T.G., she'd had mixed success with her endeavours. She'd started with clumsily draped saris, string-hoppers (more string than hopper, my mother would whisper to me) and an impressive collection of adorned wooden elephants. But it had been the 1970's, and she'd soon become distracted with bold Indian fabrics which she fashioned into long, flowing kaftans and, for special occasions, a selection of Nehru jackets heavy with embroidery. She had taken sitar lessons and dabbled in meditation. Eventually she moved on from the subcontinent and, like some 16th century Dutch explorer, she'd slowly plundered her way northward through the rest of Asia. My sister and I loved it of course - the shiny golden Buddhas, ornate Malaysian puppets, a Bonsai corner - her

house was like the Asian wing at a museum we'd visited on a school excursion, only this was a museum where we could play with the exhibits. She'd even let us wear her old outfits. My favourite was the green kimono. Irene had been determined to stick out and my mother, in her American jeans, had been determined to blend in.

After Mum died, our trips to Canberra grew further and further apart. And as we got older, my sister and I looked forward to them less and less. The only good thing about those trips was the chance to sit uninterrupted in the back seat playing Donkey Kong on my Game & Watch. Irene's eclectic taste had become embarrassing.

It was easy to spot Irene's house as we drove up. People were milling about solemnly outside, it was as if the house had spilled over with grief. I walked in behind my father, who nodded at faces that were unfamiliar to me.

"Make sure you introduce me," I whispered to the back of his head but it was so loud in there that he wouldn't have heard me. I remembered clinging to his leg as a child, wishing that I would be swallowed up in his stride. I tried staying close so I wouldn't lose him in the crowd but with each step he seemed to move a little further ahead of me.

I squeezed my way through huddled conversations, mumbling my apologies as I went. Women in their white and gently coloured saris stepped aside to let me through, and I smiled awkwardly in return. I was out of place in my dark funeral clothes and ghost-thin voice.

My mother had never felt at home in this kind of

setting. When she arrived in Australia she shed her cultural garb as quickly as my sister and I forgot our native tongue. It had been all or nothing, and she chose nothing. Secretly I had been proud of her for her choice.

I had been relieved that it wasn't my mother picking me up from school in a sari. But the fabric, as frail as a feather, had belied the strength of its wearer. A defiant attachment to the past, and a pride borne of being an outsider, that I realised had been lost on me as a child.

I saw Irene across the room. She was seated quietly, surrounded by a group of women who were having an animated conversation around her. My father must have seen her too because I could see him quickly making his way towards her. I hung back.

Irene rose as she saw my father approaching. The women made way for her as she left them, barely pausing in their conversation. There was only a moment for a greeting between them before the tears started to flow. My father touched her shoulder, and led her by the elbow towards the kitchen. I needed a drink.

"Who are you?"

Startled, I realised that the woman in front of me must have thought that I was staring at her all this time.

I am not sure how to explain myself, so apologise for staring. She dismisses my apology with a wave of her fingers.

"That's not what I meant. I said who are you? Who are your parents?"

"I'm Premnathan and Suri's daughter."

"Is that Premnathan from Sydney?"

"Yes."

"Ahhh." A hundred pathways were forming in her mind. This was the real information super-highway. Across generations and continents, connections were being made at a depth and speed that would make Google envious. I waited eagerly to see what would come out at the other end. "I remember your mother. She had a pretty face."

"Yes, that was her."

"But she died."

I nodded, it turns out beauty is no guarantee against death.

"She used to wear Western dress, didn't she?"

I tried to swallow a giggle but it came out sounding like a snort. It didn't matter, the woman didn't seem to notice.

"Are you the doctor daughter or the other one?"

"The other one." I have to get away before I start laughing. A pretty face; Western dress; a doctor daughter and another one. My mother's life in Tweets.

My mother would have found that hilarious. "Do you know where I could get a drink?"

"There are drinks in the dining room. But," she looked around before lowering her voice, "if you want a stiff drink, I found some in the kitchen."

I laughed before I remembered where I was. The woman joined in too and asked me to bring back a whisky sour for her.

The kitchen was empty except for Irene. She was bent over the kitchen sink staring out the window into the garden. The garden was in the style of a Balinese resort and I again had to stop myself from laughing. I could see my Dad pacing outside, alone among the palms and teak, dragging on his cigarette. Irene smiled as soon as she saw me. The last time she smiled at me like that was when I was wearing the green kimono.

She hitched up her sari and tugged down on the blouse that was creeping up her midriff.

"I never could get the hang of these things. No wonder Suri never wanted to wear the buggers."

Irene squeezed me tight, and I felt the tension easing from me. I shouldn't have stayed away for so long. From Uncle T.G. and Irene. From all of this.

Irene stepped back and stared at my face for so long that I thought she had forgotten to breathe.

"Your eyes are just like Prem's." She said it to herself, more air than words. In that moment, she breathed out and her smile returned. She pulled me over to the table and made me sit down beside her.

"So tell me what you've been up to all these years! It's been too long-" But her words were lost in the sound of glass breaking.

Irene dropped my hand and walked over to a man who had stumbled into the kitchen

"Ted? Ted. You've had too much to drink. Maybe you should lie down?"

Ted. Irene's little brother. I remembered a neater looking version of him from some of Uncle T.G.'s parties.

"I'm not drunk! And I'm not staying here-"

"Ted! Don't leave like this. Just stay here. Sleep it off. David won't be sleeping in his old room tonight. You can stay in there –"

But Ted brushed off his sister's offer with a shove of his hand.

"It's all rubbish. All of it! All this hypocrisy. How can you stand it? Why were you the only one who couldn't see him for what he was?"

"Ted-"

"He was a womaniser Irene! How come you can't face that? All the time, he was looking at other women-"

"No-"

"All the time Irene! All the bloody time-"

"It's not true-"

The two of them were getting louder and I didn't know where to look or what to do. I was so caught up in looking but not looking that I didn't notice Dad come through the door. He walked up to Ted and spun him around to face Dad. Then he said something to Ted that I couldn't hear, but it was enough to make Ted's shoulders sag and his eyes drop to the floor. Ted shuffled out the door, and Irene didn't follow him. She inched back to the table and sat down next to me again.

She didn't look at me and she didn't say a word. Dad walked over and laid a hand on her shoulder.

"He didn't cheat on you Irene. He loved you. He only loved you. I know that for a fact."

Irene didn't respond. She didn't even cry.

Dad gave me a look and I knew it was time to go. I went to kiss Irene on the cheek, but she was looking down, just staring at her hands, and I realised that I'd been there too long already.

***

We drove in silence until we reached Goulburn.
But that was okay. We were both treading water.
We stopped for coffee and a meal at a roadside diner.
"My treat," Dad said.
Over the roast dinner special, my father chose to
throw me a lifeline.
"Ted was wrong about T.G. He was not a womaniser.
He only ever loved one woman." He busied himself
with scraping the gravy off his pumpkin. "But it
wasn't Irene."
The words hung there. This time I grabbed at them,
but with no satisfaction.
"Is that what he told you in his letter?"
Dad nodded. "He told me. He finally told me."
"Who was she?"
"It doesn't matter. No one you knew."
And he was right. It didn't matter, not to me.
We'd finally shared something, and despite the grief
it had caused to Irene, I was silently and selfishly
grateful for what it had brought to me. We ate in
silence for a long time, broken finally by the laughter
of two young men who walked into the diner and sat
at the table beside us.
Their laughter must have been infectious because Dad
started to laugh. A big throaty laugh that reminded me
of Christmas. He wiped at his eyes and leaned in
towards me.
"You know, when your Uncle T.G. was a young man,
he used to travel 60 miles for a dance? Can you
believe that?"
My chest began to tighten.

"'Hang it!' he would say. Sometimes he managed to convince me to come along. He had this Daimler - you know he never bought anything local - and we would ..."

He didn't need to finish the story for me. I already knew how it would turn out.

9

THE SONS OF ESAU
BY MICHAEL PRYOR

When the phone call came in the middle of the night, the first thing that Roy Paxman did was reach for Marie to reassure her. He'd done it every time the phone rang like that for thirty-four years now, even though she hadn't been there for the last sixteen.
He answered. They asked him to come in, politely.
He said he would.
He dressed in the dark, not wanting to wake Marie who wasn't there. He knotted his tie, peered out of the window at the rain, tugged on his coat, and left.
He didn't shave.
Roy Paxman was a methodical man. After Marie had left, he'd examined himself. He'd taken took large sheets of butcher's paper and drew up columns, detailing her complaints as best as he could remember them. He'd studied them and decided that she'd been right, especially about the item at the top.
He didn't listen.

Paxman couldn't argue, not with butcher's paper.

He never listened to her, not properly. He caught the gist of what she was saying, sometimes, but his mind was often elsewhere. The job?

Paxman didn't shy from the evidence. He made changes. Not to lure her back. He had no illusions about that. She never contacted him in any way. He could have used friends in the force to track her down, but high up in his list of failings had been treating people like criminals even when they weren't, so he didn't.

No, he didn't change to get her back. He made changes as penance.

He drove. He kept his hands light on the wheel, tapping time to the windscreen wipers.

Security at the station was another thing that had changed. When he started you could park right out the front and walk in. Not anymore. Paxman had to show his identification. The fresh-faced youngster manning the gatehouse scanned it from behind thick glass. He nodded at Paxman as if he hadn't seen him before.

The new Chief Inspector was at least ten years younger than Paxman. He was lean, fit and his hair had only just started going grey. 'An ugly one for you,

Paxman.'

'Has he seen a solicitor?'

'Says he doesn't want one. He wants to talk. Should make things easier, then?'

'It can,' Paxman said. 'It can make things harder, too.'

'Ah.'

'He's in Room 3?'

'They said that was the room you preferred.'
'It is.'
Two constables were standing either side of the door.
One of them barely awake. The other was pale in the
dim corridor. Paxman knew him. 'Bourtsos.'
'Inspector Paxman. Sir.' Bourtsos gave Paxman a
folder. He glanced at the closed door. 'Nail him, will
you sir?'

***

Paxman stood with the closed door at his back. The
manacled prisoner, with no door at his back, sat at the
small table in the middle of the room.
He wasn't a talker, Paxman immediately decided, not
in the usual sense. Talkers blurted, couldn't help
themselves. They'd never just sit there, smiling. And
it wasn't the "I've got a secret" smile. It was a
tolerant smile that Paxman didn't like at all.
All killers were different. Some were angry, some
were deluded, some flitted wildly between extremes.
Paxman didn't try to categorise them. He took them
as they came and did his job.
He listened to their confession. Sometimes he was
avuncular, sometimes he was their friend, sometimes
he was their stern punisher. Whatever they needed,
Paxman provided. He gave them permission to
confess.
He dared them to confess. He conspired with them to
confess.
Everything he heard was good for him. He was
horrified, sickened, shocked, but every sordid story

was useful. It hurt, he deserved it, and he was able to do some good because of it.

Paxman drew up his chair.

Some of those brought to this room thought that their deeds would make them glamorous. Paxman knew otherwise. The perpetrators had embarked on a journey from a life of grubby squalor to one even more sordid than they could imagine.

Paxman wasn't worried for his safety. He was big enough and experienced enough to handle just about anyone. In this case, though, he was sure he'd have no trouble.

The man across the table was small. He had the sort of build that Paxman imagined came with hollow bones. His nose was sharp and beaky. His eyes were deep-set and dark. His hair was thick, black and carefully combed back. An old-fashioned odour wafted across the table, sweet and heavy like clover. *Hair oil.* Paxman was surprised. He hadn't smelled genuine hair oil for years – decades, most likely. He remembered his father standing in front of the bathroom mirror. He'd always turn his head from side to side to check all was in place. His head gleamed after he applied his hair oil.

A document in the folder told Paxman that Maurice Sleysholder was fifty-three. Not a member of the hair oil generation. It was an affectation, and affectations could be insights into character.

Paxman closed the folder. Was this important or was it a distraction? The man was well-groomed. It could indicate a level of obsession.

'Mr Sleysholder, I'm Detective Inspector Paxman.'

Paxman turned on the recorder. 'You don't mind that we record this interview, do you?' He kept his voice gentle.

'Of course not. I won't be here long, anyway.'

Paxman nodded. Reality wasn't a sphere in which most of his interviewees operated.

The man's voice was firm and direct. No cowering, no dawning realisation that things weren't turning out as he would have wished. No threats, no tears, no overwhelmed silence.

Businesslike it is, then.

Sleysholder had both hands laced together on the table in front of him. He nodded at Paxman, lifted them, and pointed with both forefingers. 'I like your tie.'

Paxman took a pencil from his jacket pocket. 'Thanks. I do too. I bought a dozen of them.'

'That's the sort of firmness of mind I appreciate.'

A meeting of equals, then.

'Mr Sleysholder, I'm sure you appreciate the situation we have here.'

'I should. I'm responsible.'

Paxman opened the folder again. Maurice Sleysholder had indeed been invisible to the authorities all his life. A quiet, law-abiding citizen who had killed sixteen people.

Why?

Paxman studied the man while appearing to look down. He wore a dark blue blazer and an open-necked shirt that was startlingly white and crisp, even at this hour.

Vanity. Stroke his vanity.

'I'm glad to hear you're accepting responsibility, Mr Sleysholder. Most people in your position wouldn't.'

'I can't understand that.'

'Which is an entirely rational approach, but I've had dozens sitting in just the seat you're in now, claiming that other people did it, that they weren't in their right mind, or that society made them.'

Sleysholder shrugged. It was a quick, decisive movement, almost entirely in his shoulders, leaving his elbows and hands motionless. 'They may not have had the necessity I did.'

Paxman sometimes likened his interviews to mining for gold. Hammering away at a rock face, moving tonnes of dross, always alert for a glimmer that might mean riches.

'I see. Your actions were necessary?'

Sleysholder's eyebrows moved up and in. Finely shaped, they were too, Paxman noticed. 'Of course they were necessary. I wouldn't have undertaken them if it weren't.'

Easy now.

'Sixteen people. That's quite an undertaking. Perhaps you'd like to tell me about them?

Sleysholder pursed his lips. 'I'd rather not. It's not something I want to dwell on.'

Paxman made a note about Sleysholder's apparent squeamishness.

Let's look at the necessity, then.

Paxman glanced at the single barred window. Rain battered it. The weather didn't often come from that direction.

'Lovely night,' Sleysholder said.

'For ducks.'

'And other things.'

Paxman caught this one. 'You like the dark?'

'Me? No, I'm a day person.'

'But other things like the dark.'

'It's their home.'

Ah.

'Such as?' Paxman asked.

'You don't have to shave often, do you?'

Paxman rolled with it. He'd had far worse non sequiturs.

Self-disclosure time.

Self-disclosure was a useful tool in his questioning. Give a little to gain a great deal. 'Not really. Shaving every day is as much a habit as a necessity.'

'I thought so. You're a smooth man.'

Paxman wrote down the phrase. Then he underlined it. *Smooth man.*

'You could say that,' Paxman said. 'It has its advantages.'

'Of course it does.' Sleysholder smiled broadly.

'But you must have discovered the antipathy it arouses from others.'

Us and them. Go with him.

Paxman grunted. 'You wouldn't believe the number of times I've been passed over for promotion because of it.' He grunted again. 'They always get the inside running.'

'You have to understand, it's only natural. Since time immemorial, I think the phrase is, the smooth man has been the lesser.'

'I take it you're not a smooth man?'

Sleysholder straightened. Paxman could see the chest hair bristling in the open neck of his shirt. 'I should say not. I am one of the proudest of the Sons of Esau.'

'Esau?' Paxman wrote it down.

'"Behold, Esau my brother is a hairy man, and I am a smooth man."' Sleysholder looked at the ceiling. 'Genesis, chapter 27, verse 11.'

'The Sons of Esau are hairy men.' Paxman was on his way. He'd opened the door and Sleysholder's delusions were tumbling out.

Sleysholder laughed. 'We are. Vital, vigorous and virile. In the age old struggle between the hairy men and the smooth men, the Sons of Esau are the natural winners.'

Paxman shuffled through the documents in his folder. The sixteen victims stared out at him. Bald descriptions. Death reduced to GPS coordinates.

'So you killed sixteen smooth men because of this struggle.'

Sleysholder went to cross his arms on his chest, but was confounded by his handcuffs. He shook his head. 'I thought you were quicker than that.'

'I'm sorry.'

'You, and the other meddlers have interrupted my work. You've brought me in here for the dispatching of some unfortunate Sons of Esau.'

'You killed hairy men? Your own kind?'

Primly: 'It was necessary, as I said.'

'I'm sorry. You've lost me.'

The lights flickered. A long second or two later, thunder shook night. Paxman wrinkled his nose at the smell of ozone in the air.

'I'm not insane,' Sleysholder said quietly once the echoes had died away.

Honesty.

'I don't know if you are or you aren't. Most people will assume you are, because of what you've done.'

'The smooth men will lead the outcry, I have no doubt. They have me where they want me.'

'You're in no danger here.'

'I know that.' Sleysholder sighed. 'It's embarrassing, really, all of this.'

Sixteen murders – embarrassing? 'In what way?'

'I'm afraid that you've become embroiled in one of the typical internal squabbles among the Sons of Esau.

We do try to keep these things from the public.'

'I imagine you do.'

'And this wasn't my eliminating rivals, if that's what you're thinking.'

'It's a natural conclusion.'

'And a fine one, for a smooth man to reach.'

Paxman had steeled himself not to react to invective, or bluster, or threats. He hadn't had much experience in remaining impassive in the face of being patronised.

He managed.

Flatter.

'I'm guessing that some sort of power struggle was involved.'

Sleysholder almost preened. 'And that, good sir, is very close to the point. Movements among the mighty.'

Paxman spread the post-mortem photographs in front of him. *Careful here.* 'A power struggle that meant you had to remove their eyelashes as well as-'
What was his word? 'Dispatching them.'
'I had enough ordinary hair. I needed the eyelashes.'
It made no sense at all. Paxman found Sleysholder's details.
'You're a hairdresser.'
Sleysholder made a face. 'I'm not a hairdresser. I am a barber.'
Paxman had a sudden, disconcerting image of Sleysholder with a razor in his hand. 'All barbers are Sons of Esau?'
'Some Sons of Esau are barbers. We are special. Part of a long and noble tradition.'
Paxman nodded and made some more notes.
No-one else would have found his notes useful. They were more impressionistic than representational.
Details that caught his eye, thoughts, reminders.
Here, Paxman was constructing Sleysholder.
Despite the details of his delusion, he was falling into a typical pattern. Sleysholder was special, a man apart.
Not just special, but a special group within a special group. Special, with rules of their own.
Rules that allowed him to do what he did.
Paxman studied the photographs again. He felt as if he had one foot on a pier and one in a boat about to leave.
'You needed these eyelashes for something Important?'
Impatience. 'Of course it was important. I wouldn't dispatch Sons of Esau over something trivial. I

wouldn't even dispatch smooth men over something trivial.'

Validate him. Use his words.

'They were necessary,' Paxman said.

A smile hovered on Sleysholder's lips as if unsure it belonged there. 'That's right. It took me some time to divine the correct method.'

'The correct method for what?'

Mistake.

Sleysholder frowned at the bluntness of Paxman's interest. He sat back in his chair and gazed at the ceiling. 'The Sons of Esau are powerful.'

Paxman felt like sighing. He'd been close, but now Sleysholder was off on his lunatic flights of fancy again. More thunder overhead, close enough that it sounded like artillery.

'They're in control,' Paxman said, gently encouraging.

Sleysholder glanced at the rain on the window. 'We are in governments everywhere – overtly or covertly. We dominate the entertainment industry. We manipulate the international financial system for their own ends.'

Of course you do. 'You're everywhere,' Paxman said with a calculated touch of bitterness.

Sleysholder dropped his gaze and met Paxman's - and Paxman saw the man capable of killing sixteen people just for their eyelashes. 'Oh, yes. We keep you smooth ones in your place. After all, we are the natural leaders. We are more intelligent, more decisive, stronger.' Sleysholder dropped his voice and looked at Paxman slyly. 'We take your women, too.'

Sleysholder went on, recounting how hairy men were exempt from the rules of society and how they were the true rulers of the world, but Paxman hardly heard him.

Marie.

Paxman had framed his life neatly. His work. His home. His long ago youth. He'd ordered them neatly, thought about them just so, was comfortable with the way they were arranged.

Marie had been in a neat frame. Sad and full of regrets, but neat like all the others. It had been painful.

He was ready to admit he'd been far from blameless. She'd left him, was how he always put it. It was as if she were a ship, sailing off into foggy waters where he lost sight of her.

Except it hadn't been like that. His framing had been careful. It omitted.

Sometimes, Paxman thought, truth was sacrificed in the need to go on. *No*, he corrected, *not sacrificed. Reframed.*

Marie hadn't left, with all the vagueness and uncertainty that implied. She'd gone off with another man.

It pained Paxman. Sleysholder's insinuation had rocked him, sent him off balance, but it had been a lucky shot. Dominance struggles between smooth and hair men? Life wasn't that ridiculous.

In another interview, years ago, Paxman had managed to engage a glassy-eyed subject by querying him on technique. The killer had brightened for a moment. Then he shrugged. 'If you keep stabbing long enough, you'll eventually hit something vital.'

Paxman wanted to bring this awry interview back onto the tracks. He was helped by a mighty crash of thunder. It was followed by the rain intensifying so much that speaking was impossible.

It was the pause he needed.

Sleysholder smiled at Paxman and waggled his head from side to side. A clown.

Paxman put both hands on the table lest he float away.

The din subsided. Sleysholder picked up again. Calmly. 'I'm planning to become the effective leader of the Sons of Esau.'

'Go on.'

Paxman could have kicked himself. It was a lame response. He must be tired.

He scratched a note. Sleysholder wasn't using the past tense.

'You understand, of course,' Sleysholder said, 'that the Sons of Esau have a supremo, a chief?'

'It would make sense.' Paxman's tongue didn't snap off at the roots. It was used to lying in the pursuit of justice.

'My plan is to replace the current leader with one of my own making.'

'You'll be the puppet master? The power behind the throne?'

'In a manner of speaking.' He pursed his lips before going on. 'My plan is to make a new Lord of the Hairy Men. It will be under my control. Riches, power and admiration will be mine.'

Paxman touched his cheek with a hand.

Sleysholder had veered from lunatic territory to the outright bizarre. 'I'm having trouble following this.'

The lights flickered, stuttered, then reasserted themselves. For an instant, disturbing shadows had flitted across the table, the documents, the manacles on Sleysholder's hands.

'Of course,' Sleysholder said. 'But at least you listen. No-one else has.'

Oh yes, Paxman thought wearily. *I listen, and the pain is good.*

He asked a question he never could have imagined coming from his lips: 'How do you make a Lord of the Hairy Men?'

Sleysholder leaned close, putting both hands and both elbows on the table in front of him. 'By using the most magical part of humanity, the part that grows while we live, that is renewed while we exist, that marks us for what we are.'

'You're talking about hair.'

'In my mundane job, I accumulated much hair. I experimented, but did not know how to bind it and make it into a Lord of the Hairy Men. I discovered that certain members of the brotherhood of barbers are the custodians of this knowledge. I travelled, persevered, found them and learned.'

Visions of a mystical league of barber monks came to Paxman and made him momentarily dizzy. 'They taught you willingly?'

'After a time, they were willing.'

Leave it.

Sleysholder rattled his handcuffs on the table. 'I found out from them why my experiments hadn't worked. I was missing a crucial ingredient.'

Light flashed, brilliant white, through the window.

Paxman blinked, dazzled, purple spots swimming in his vision. Before he could raise a hand to rub his eyes, the biggest thunderclap of all made the night explode.

The lights went out.

In the darkness, Paxman's ears rang. He heard Sleysholder's voice, quiet and unperturbed. 'My failures came because my creatures needed to see before they were complete. They needed the hair of the eyes.'

The voice wasn't coming from across the table. Paxman didn't move. He strained to listen over the thumping of his heart. He could hear shouts coming from somewhere in the building.

'Who would have thought that eyelashes were so important?' Sleysholder went on, lost in the blackness.

'Or that I'd need so many?'

The emergency lights came on, dim and yellow. Paxman relaxed. Sleysholder had backed himself into the far corner. In the jaundiced emergency lights, the scene was familiar. A reluctant prisoner, unwilling to cooperate.

Paxman rubbed his face with both hands. He kept one eye on Sleysholder. He shifted all the documents into the folder. He closed it. 'Time to go.'

Sleysholder grinned, madly. 'Not with you, I'm afraid. Someone's coming to pick me up me.'

'Have it your way.'

Paxman winced as he climbed to his feet. Good pain. He'd earned and deserved it and it was making him better.

Still with one eye on Sleysholder, he thumped on the door. 'Need some help in here.'

Nothing.

He thumped again.

Nothing, except for a heavy clumping sound approaching. Then rustling, whispering from the corridor.

The smell of wet dog.

Paxman was afraid.

In the gloom, Sleysholder spread his manacled hands.

Paxman didn't take his gaze from the lunatic. He reached around behind him. He opened the door.

'*Behold*,' Sleysholder breathed. '*Esau, my brother, is a hairy man.*'

Paxman turned to face the source of the rustling behind him.

Or is Sleysholder a hairy man? We have our attractions.

Paxman studied Sleysholder's face. The man's face was almost unnaturally hairless. Was the man one of those whose motivation was a grudge against humanity? Had he rationalised his rage at being overlooked, spurned or abused by blaming it on being part of an imagined minority?

One that he assumed Paxman was a member of?

'What did you do?'

'I experimented.'

The simple response, with all the seriousness of a chemist, was enough to make Paxman wish he hadn't eaten, ever.

He shuffled the photographs to give himself time.

Each person had been killed in a different way - unusual in a case like this - but the eyelashes had been carefully removed from each.

'And that's why you needed sixteen ... donors?' Paxman finally managed.

'Sixteen?' Sleysholder repeated, vaguely. 'I was never much good with numbers.'

Paxman restrained himself again. They were people, not numbers.

10

FIVE DEGREES FROM HAPPINESS
BY KERRY BROWN

"Get away from my jewels or I'll blow your bloody head off!" the woman screamed in a strong Russian accent. She looked up with blood shot eyes and a toothless snarl. A familiarity lingered between us as I froze and looked at her, open mouthed and wide-eyed.

In her hand she had produced a revolver. Well, what I thought to be a revolver, I really wasn't too au-fait with guns and their differing labels. Her hand shook desperately in an attempt to hold steady as she directed the gun at my temple.

It was about 11.30pm and my friend Kyle, another fellow named Taj, that we had only just met three hours previously, and I had stopped off at the local gas station to fill up with fuel and pick up some beer. Strange I know, but yes you can get beer from a service station in Hollywood. Just as easily as you can buy a gun across the counter at the local Wal-Mart store!

It was a hot and sweltering night. I glanced at my phone. It was five degrees hotter than when I had looked at it an hour ago. The servo was quiet. Two pumps and a small pay station idly awaited late night customers. The attendant could be seen inside through his bulletproof glass. A bland looking man with acne scars and his index finger shoved deeply into his left nostril, sat in a swivel chair. He was picking, swiveling, swigging on a coke and reading a comic all at once.

"See, men can multi task!" I jest, poking my friend Kyle in the ribs.

Kyle was English. He was an intelligent drunk. Reckons he had five different University degrees back home. He was sick of studying and decided to travel for a while, before earning back some of the money he had spent on fees. I'd met him lying on the floor of the backpackers I was both staying and working at.

I had come overseas to discover my 'true' self. I am Australian of Turkish decent with little knowledge or understanding of my blended heritage.

I was one of five children. Being the youngest made me the fifth child. We had spent our entire lives at 5 Degrees Avenue, just five degrees and 55 kilometres north west of Sydney. For as long as I could remember, I had received $5 a week for pocket money from my mother and to date I had been in five serious relationships, all of which failed due to my undying love with Minus Five Degrees.

Minus Five Degrees is a bar in Sydney central,

entirely made of ice. The bar is ice, the glasses are made of ice and the bar you sat at was also made of ice.

My girlfriends had taken me there for my 18th birthday.

I fell in love with the place immediately. Something about drinking vodka in minus five degrees made the experience so much more enjoyable. Previous to this and I hadn't really liked vodka. However, the crispness of the air with the refreshing burn of vodka as it rushed past my palate seemed to heighten my senses. It made me feel alive.

I would drag my girlfriends back there with me at every available opportunity. At first I told myself it was the novelty of the bar. The dressing up in fur coats and thick woolen hats made a pleasant change to hitting the nightclub scene in a mini dress. I felt less vulnerable.

Less targeted by the trawling single men of Sydney. It wasn't long before I started going there for a drink on my own. I thought of it as my calling, considering my reoccurring affiliation with the number five. This number seemed to pop up continuously in my life and had become somewhat of a crutch that I used to make important decisions. Sounds odd, I know. But it became my security blanket.

The best thing about the Minus Five bar was on a Thursday night at 5pm all vodka shots were five dollars. There couldn't have been a clearer sign!

So that is where my girlfriends and each of my five failed boyfriends could always find me. Inside the bar, I was usually coherent and sociable. It was when I left that it hit me. The fresh air and removal of the fur coat would smack me in the head with a rush of nausea and dizziness, rendering me incoherent and often violent.

My boyfriends left me and soon, so did my friends. One night when sitting at the bar a lady came up beside me and downed three shots of Russian vodka before she even sat down. Over $5 specials we became 'blindly' acquainted.

She told me of her struggle with the bottle and how it had crept up on her so quietly that she had missed the red flags that were being waved so obviously in front of her face. She had accidentally filled her baby's bottle with vodka instead of water and had embarrassed her husband on his award night by falling asleep under his table during the speeches, snoring so loudly so that nobody could hear him, despite his microphone. She had seen a glimpse of herself in the future through the eyes of her alcoholic father. Unfortunately, by this point she had gone too far. She had lost her husband, her children, her job and her self-respect. She now drank at the Minus Five Bar because the vodka, along with the sub-zero temperatures, helped numb both the mental and physical pain she felt.

I left the bar that night with a clarity and realization of where I was. I needed to change before any red flags were waved.

I decided to take a leap of faith and travel - alone, away from the history and threat of the bottle. I felt invincible. I believed that the answer to whatever questions I had in life would be answered abroad.

I had no plan, except that I would not visit Russia. I was going to travel five degrees at a time. If that meant I was going to land in the middle of the ocean then I would make it a multiple of five. Everyone knows about the theory of six degrees of separation but I believe in five. It brings us one step closer to each other in an ever increasingly denser world. We are living in a shrinking universe. My belief is that the more we search, the closer our past, present and future begin to merge and that somewhere in that desperate search to find out where we came from and who we are, we ultimately get a glance at who we will become in the future.

So, I started my journey in Sydney, Australia travelling twenty- five degrees East to the North Island of New Zealand. From here I island hopped and meandered in multiples of five until reaching Hollywood, California – the city of dreams.

I had managed to pick up a job as a cleaner at the Hollywood Chalets. It wasn't fancy, like the name suggests. The rooms were more like broom closets jam packed with bunk beds in an effort to cram as many backpackers as possible into them.

I worked for four hours a day in return for food and board. No green card, meant no cash.

My job was to go into the chalets each morning, empty bins and vacuum what little space was left between beds and baggage, and on one particular morning – a body. I opened the door of Chalet 5 to be greeted with a stench of bourbon and body odour like nothing words can even begin to describe. My nostril hairs curled up and I held my hand over my mouth. It wasn't a smell that made me nauseas. It was a smell that made me weak. I was weak with the desire to soak up every fume. I wanted to roll myself in it.

I took one step forward, tripping on a pile of dirty laundry and fell flat on my face. I had landed face down, eye to eye with Kyle who was dribbling happily onto the carpet, naked. I struggled to stand, kicking the bourbon bottle that lay next to him on the floor.

The bottle spun around quickly as if it was performing on queue. I watched it wearily as it started to slow and reached out to grab it and throw it into my trolley. It circled slowly and eventually stopped with its neck pointing accusingly about five degrees to the right from me.

"Wahoo!" Kyle screamed from his pile pillow.

"It's you lovely lady. Take your shoes off!" He lifted his head sleepily and grinned before collapsing into another dreamtime.

I ignored him, quickly grabbed the bottle and threw it into the rubbish bag before I sealed my lips on its slender neck. I proceeded to vacuum around Kyle. He didn't move.

From that point on Kyle nicknamed me Sadie. At first, he repulsed me. His greasiness and sour slur each morning sickened me. Admittedly, it was the green monster inside me that hated him.

Unfortunately our morning meetings became a ritual. I would vacuum around him as best I could and he would throw vile inappropriate comments at me from the floor.

This all seemed to change soon after the concept of Free Beer Night began. In an effort to make cultures mix, the Chalets had designed 'Friday Night Free Beer'.

It was a great way to meet new people, swap stories and retain youth in our own form of liquid formaldehyde.

At first I absconded, seeking refuge in my room. But week after week, it became rather lonely removed from the laughter and jovial chants coming from the beer shed. Eventually I gave in and wandered over. I thought I was strong enough to limit myself. It had been, after all, five months. I was only thankful it wasn't vodka.

I started off as a slow drinker, one beer a night, happy to be basking in the keg of multi-culture. Soon enough though, Friday night wasn't enough. Money was pooled amongst the regulars to re-enact our own idea of 'Free Beer Night' and the solidarity it brought despite language barriers, political views or cultural status. Kyle and I were part of this group. Truth be told we were its founders.

We argued incessantly about the temperature of the beer. Kyle, being from the UK always wanted it five degrees warmer, and I always wanted it five degrees colder. This was one argument we could never settle. Slowly, our common friend of liquid amber formed a familiar river between us, of which we were both happy to swim in. Kyle and I became friends. Drinking friends.

We would sing in harmony during karaoke and break into the kitchen to make late night plastic cheese and Tabasco Sauce toasted sandwiches. Kyle was my soul mate. He understood me.

Each morning I would rise with the familiar taste of stale hops and cigarettes in the back of my throat. I would reach for my diary and start to write down the fabulous events of the night before. Oh, what memories I would have. The people I was meeting! The fun and laughter we had shared. Once a week I would send a postcard home telling my Mum and Dad of the adventures I was having. In truth I was telling them the tales of others I had heard over a bottle of beer. But I didn't care, I was happy. I was appreciated. I made others laugh.

By 11pm, we had usually run out of beer. Our tongues were beginning to gather fur and our conversation was starting to dry up. A mission to replenish our social comfort always sent us off in search of more to drink. Tonight was no different. This is how we ended up at the gas station.

"I'll let you know I have always been able to multi task – I can drink and drive!" Kyle sung back at me as he walked off towards the gas station shop.

Kyle and Taj went inside to get the beer and pay for the gas while I chose to stop and admire the jewellery stand of a homeless woman set up outside the gas station store.

I guessed she was homeless. Her hands were filthy with roadside grime and the clothes she wore stank of urine and stale beer. I looked harder, beneath the layers of dirt that covered her and from underneath her straw hat I saw a pretty face with defined cheekbones, arched eyebrows and full lips. I smiled politely.

The stall was nothing spectacular. The table was made up of an old door balanced precariously on two rickety wooden chairs. A makeshift tablecloth had been spread out - yellow rubber duckies printed onto a plastic curtain. Mould stains could be seen dotted along the print.

The pieces were all homemade and quite simple. Buttons thread onto string, earrings made out of bottle tops and bracelets made out of o-rings. I liked the idea of buying a piece that would ultimately help someone out. The rawness of the jewellery fitted perfectly with the idea of living free, experiencing life to it's fullest and immortalising a moment in time.

I had honest intentions of buying a piece and chatted casually with the woman about her work.

"Can you watch my store for me love?" she asked. "Just need to use the bathroom."

"Sure," I happily obliged, full of carefree, backpacker trust.

The woman was gone for about five minutes before she emerged from the toilets and carefully swaggered her way back towards the table. She sat down in her chair without looking up, seemingly unaware of my lingering presence. Her eyes had glazed over and she tried to focus as her floating aura swam in and out of view. She had rolled up her left sleeve and fresh droplets of blood could be seen on the inner crease of her arm.

I picked up a piece of beer glass wrapped tightly in a length of wire, trying to casually ignore the obvious. I was about to ask how much, when the woman finally looked up.

That's when the revolver appeared….straight into my face.

"Nobody steals my bloody jewels!" she screamed. "Specially not you Mika!"

She was enraged and confused. The revolver was swinging from side to side as she tried to stand and lurch across the table towards me.

I looked over my shoulder. The attendant was now inhaling a Mars Bar and a chocolate milk, this time picking his right nostril.

I opened my mouth to explain………

A screech of tyres sounded directly behind me and before I knew it I was being grabbed from behind by the scuff of my shirt and dragged into the backseat of a car. Kyle's car.

The door slammed shut and we sped off down the road. I sat there wide-eyed waiting for the sound of a bullet to ricochet of the back of the car. There was nothing.

I drank a lot of beer that night.

The next morning I awoke between Kyle and Taj, on the floor. The two of them had formed a protective barrier around me. I had sobbed so hard that night that they didn't know what else to do. So they drank, gave me drink and lay next to me.

I slowly wiggled my way out from between them and opened the bathroom door to wash my face. At first, I thought I had the wrong door, for there in front of me was a boulder. Not a small rock but a very large boulder sitting in the space that the bath used to be. Katrina, the South African girl sharing our dorm, came in behind me. "Amazing huh! Who would have thought we'd be here during an earthquake." She looked at me. "How much did you guys drink last night anyway? None of you even budged when this rock came rolling down the hill and smashing through our wall. I went and slept next door. I didn't want to be in here when the coyotes sniffed us out! They say if the hill had been five degrees steeper, that boulder would have crushed the lot of us!" She laughed as she reached out over my shoulder and grabbed her toiletry bag.

I sat down on the toilet seat and closed my eyes. I was looking directly down the barrel of a gun.

Memories of the night before came flooding back to me. I shook my head. Maybe it didn't really happen, but then again a boulder had really smashed through the bathroom door and I hadn't woken.

Anything was possible. Was this a red flag?

How did the jewellery lady know my name? Did she really scream it out? Did it really happen at all?

I put my head in my hands and leaned back against the wall. That was when I became aware of something in my pocket. It was hard and small......
and uncomfortable.

I reached in and pulled it out.......the small green piece of beer glass wrapped in wire. I still had it. Beneath the wire, upon the glass, a small inscription could be seen. I unwound the wire carefully so as to not cut myself. Scratched carefully into the glass were three letters – z. o. m. – zom.

I ran my mind through the shelves of lager and varying spirits at the bottle shop, trying to picture which brand of alcohol had the word or letters zom on it. I couldn't think of anything. I put the glass back in my pocket and went back into the bedroom to wake Kyle. It was time for a drink.

A week or two passed and the memory of the

woman at the service station was never far from my
mind. I drank in the hope that it would clarify my
thoughts. I drank in the hope to forget.

Kyle laughed at me and said I was delirious. He
said my imagination was running wild but it was a
great story to tell over drinks, so he was happy for me
to embellish. So drink we did. We drank 'til our
kidneys hurt.

One morning, as Kyle was throwing out the bottles
from the night before he picked up my piece of glass
and rolled it in his hand. "Don't remember breaking
any glass," he said, while opening up the rubbish bag
to dispose of it.

I lunged across the bed towards him like a woman
obsessed. "Don't throw it out!" I screamed at him.
Kyle tossed the glass towards me." Sheez…. don't get
your knickers in a knot love. Have a drink. Chill out a
little. It's just glass."

That night I caught a cab to the bottle shop around the
corner and spent three hours looking up and down the
aisles trying to match my piece of glass and it's letters
to something on the shelf. I figured I had overstayed
my welcome when the security guard came over and
asked if there was anything he could do to help me. I
grabbed a bottle of vodka, smiled politely and left.

It sounds insane that a piece of glass would have so
much of a pull over me. You may think it has to do
with my love of the bottle. But I'm not a drunk. I can
let go.

What I can't let go of is the 'glass lady' as I had come
to call her. It was beyond me. So, one night I decided
to take matters into my own hands. I borrowed Kyle's

car and told him I was going to fill it up on account of how much I had been using it.

I had no intention telling him where I was going.

I pulled the car up in one of the spare parking bays to the side of the servo shop. Inside, the same monotonous attendant sat, swiveling, shoveling and slurping. I got out of the car and closed the door quietly.

I looked over towards the toilet block where the 'glass lady' had her stall sitting previously. Damn, it was gone.

I walked over to the shop window and tapped on the glass. The attendant pressed a button and spoke to me, disinterested. "Yeah, what ya want?" He didn't look up from his comic.

"I'm um, I'm not here for fuel..." He rolled his eyes and flopped his head to the side looking at me over the top of his nose.

"So?" he spat.

"So, I was wanting to ask you about the women that had a jewellery stall set up over there a couple of weeks ago."

"Dunno what ya talkin' 'bout," he went back to his comic.

"She was right there. Selling jewellery out of bits and pieces. She looked homeless, possibly Russian?"

"Listen love. I don't know nothin' that you're talkin' about. So I can't help ya."

I grunted a meaningless thankyou at the attendant and walked towards the toilet block.

The smell of the block was rancid and foul from metres away. I held my nose and entered the toilets

warily. The light above flickered yellow and white, strobing against stained walls and cement floors.
In the corner, near the basin, I could see someone lying flat across the floor.
"Hello! Are you there?" I whispered. Of course she was bloody there you fool.
I crept closer using my lighter to guide the way. The water from the tap was running and the sink clogged with paper towel was overflowing. The woman's face was wet and her hair clung to the side of her head. The grime and dirt had seemingly washed away and left her features recognisable. Around her neck hung a long silver chain. I picked it up and slid my hand along it to the end. Clasped tightly to the end of the chain was a clump of glass. It was identical to the piece in my pocket. Inscribed on the back of it were the same three letters....z o m.
I stopped and stared as I looked in to what appeared to be a reflection of myself.
At first I thought my eyes must have been playing tricks on me. I blinked a few times and knelt down closer to the body. I placed my fingers to her neck. She was dead. She was me. And she was dead.
The collar on my red shirt seemed to tighten around my neck. I was breathing fast and shallow.
I reached down and placed my hand inside her pockets frantically looking for the woman's I.D. In the bottom of her coat was a piece of paper. I unraveled it.
In front of me was an obituary. It read, Mika Yilmaz, died age 23. Found Zom (Turkish for dead drunk). Lived her life five degrees away from true happiness. Survived by her husband Kyle.

I looked down at what I was wearing. It was the shirt my mother had made me before I had left. She had made it herself and sewn it together by combining the fabrics of the Australian flag and the Turkish flag. It was cleverly patterned so I knew it's hidden sentiment.
To everyone else it was just a red shirt. To me, it was my red flag.

A PROJECT OF

THE AUSTRALIAN LITERATURE REVIEW
www.auslit.net

The goal of The Australian Literature Review is to revitalise Australian fiction, to showcase vibrant and original Australian fiction, and to assist storytellers to further develop their fiction writing skills.

Of course, this project is what it is because of the efforts of the ten authors (in alphabetical order): Kerry Brown, JJ Cooper, Belinda Dorio, Jo Hart, Rebecca James, Fleur McDonald, Michael Pryor, Sonali Rajanayagam, Sam Stephens and Michael White. A special thanks to each of you for your involvement in this project.